BEAUTIFUL ENEMY

ENEMIES #1

PIPER LAWSON

Content editing by Becca Mysoor
Line and copy editing by Cassie Roberston and Joy Editing
Cover photography by Regina Wamba

1

———

RAE

The man across the arrivals lounge in Ibiza is abrasively beautiful. The kind of attractive that could rip you in two.

Which is exactly what seeing him does to me.

Wearing a dark suit, cut close to his strong body, he carries himself with a confidence no man should possess.

No one is that right, least of all *him*.

The man in the lounge turns, calling out to a woman across the room. He's handsome, but I realize he's not the man I haven't been able to get out of my head for the past two months.

This man has dark eyes, not electrifying blue ones. He lacks the crisp British accent that reeks of boarding schools and privilege. Plus, I don't have that feeling in my gut, as if the ground is vibrating beneath my feet.

"I'm sorry, Miss Madani." The baggage clerk's bright voice drags my attention back to the counter. "Your bag was tracked from New York to Heathrow but hasn't shown on the system since."

Her words settle in, and a knot forms in my chest. "That's not possible. I need that bag."

"If we can't deliver it to you in twenty-four hours, you will be reimbursed up to five hundred euros."

I press the heels of my hands to my eyes.

Barely sleeping on the plane, then stumbling onto the next after stopping to brush my teeth and collect a Starbucks grande to get me through customs and the transfer is catching up to me.

I should've known it was a bad idea to put everything I owned in that bag.

Including my pills.

Someone bumps me from behind, and I glance back to see a string of five women in matching white minidresses. The woman at the front of the bachelorette train that was on my plane is wearing a crown and sash, and the train hollers about "one last time."

I'm the only one here *not* looking for a party.

"I understand this is disappointing. A young

woman like you, I bet you had your vacation wardrobe chosen." The woman takes in my black tank top and ripped jeans as if I'd do better to start from scratch.

"I'm not here on vacation." I shove a chunk of dark hair out of my face and feel for my crossbody bag, the computer nestled inside.

Thank fuck.

I wonder what she'd say if I told her the truth. That I'm here because I set my career on fire standing up for what I believed in and every venue that was fighting to finger me two months ago is dodging my calls.

When I leave the baggage area, the low-grade throbbing in my gut won't quit.

The company that hired me said they'd send a ride. Sure enough, by the doors is a huge man in a linen suit with graying hair. He holds a sign that says "*L. Queen.*"

"That's me." Professionally, at least. "You can call me Rae."

"No baggage?"

"I wish. What's your name?"

"Toro, señorita."

I fall into step with him as we dodge tourists and head out the double doors.

"Looks like everyone's here to party," I notice.

The people pouring out of the airport are ready to dance and drink and party their cares away.

"And you?" Toro asks.

"I'm here to help them."

I grin and slide my sunglasses onto my face, the warm air washing over me. It was spring in New York yesterday, and now it's summer in Spain.

The ocean breeze washes over me as Toro shows me to a Mercedes limo and holds open the back door.

"I'm riding up front."

Before he can argue, I pull on the passenger door and lift a book off the seat—*Eat, Pray, Love.*

"This your throwback book club pick of the week?" I set it on the dash, and my lips twitch as I cut him a look. "Don't get me wrong, I read it. Upper-middle-class blond chick searches for purpose after her divorce. Found it as relatable as you probably did. Some of us don't need an international journey to find ourselves."

I fasten my seatbelt as he pulls out of the spot.

"Then what are you doing here?"

I shift in my seat under his suddenly curious gaze. "Dream come true. You mix in Ibiza, you can work anywhere."

But this gig isn't just my big shot...

It's my last shot.

I'm twenty-four years old, and if I don't crush this residency, I might never get another chance to do for a living the one thing that makes me feel alive.

I've wanted to make electronic music since I first put on headphones in front of the computer my parents got me after a traumatic sophomore year of high school.

DJing connects me with an audience in a way that's safe and intimate at once. Unlike other performances, they don't come to watch me.

They come so I'll move them.

There's no better trip.

But the industry doesn't exactly welcome new people with open arms. I've fought with everything I have to get where I am.

Or at least where I was two months ago.

"You came alone," my driver says as we pull out of the airport, and I arch an eyebrow.

"You'd be surprised what a woman can do without a man, Toro," I tease.

I can't imagine being serious enough about a guy to have him travel with me for work.

I'm not blaming my viewpoint on divorced parents. More like every time life has gotten hard, I've found myself alone.

People leave fast when having your back costs them something.

"I have a grown daughter I haven't seen in some time. She is independent like you. That is why I'm reading the book. My wife said our daughter enjoyed it, and I would like to understand what she likes."

It's so paternal my chest tightens. "She's lucky you take an interest."

"I'm sure your parents are very proud," he says, and I swallow the hard lump that rises up my throat without responding. "I will take you to your accommodations."

"Would you take me to the club instead? I need to check on some specs." Besides, there's nothing I'll do at the villa except stress about my bag.

Toro palms the wheel like a caress. "*Debajo*. It means below."

We pass another venue on the beach side of the road. The sign marking the entrance to the outdoor club is huge, and I watch it in the passenger mirror, a shiver starting in my chest and leaving me tingling all the way down to my toes.

"That's La Mer." I sit up straighter.

People plan their entire vacations, their entire years, to join the party at one of the biggest clubs in the world.

"I'm going to play there someday."

Toro laughs. "No woman has." He shrugs at my curious look. "My daughter is into EDM."

I slide my sunglasses down and smile, feeling my ribs expand with possibility. "Tell her I'll be the first."

***

Debajo is housed beneath a resort, a fact I forgot until Toro parks around the side of the hotel and walks me to a back entrance.

The underground venue used to be popular but has seen better days, but it still picks up crowds on the long weekends in the summer—like everywhere else on the island.

Toro speaks to security in rapid-fire Spanish, and they let me in.

"Call when you are ready to go to the villa," he insists, pushing a card into my hand as I sling my crossbody bag over my shoulder.

When he's gone, I turn to survey my space.

Everything is industrial, black and chrome. Bars along either side and the stage at the far end of the floor. Booths surround the dance floor. A catwalk overhead wraps around in a balcony and cuts over the middle of the floor, partially obscured by a low, black wall—probably VIP booths.

Two guys work behind the bar, readying it for the evening ahead, while another moves boxes with a cart. None acknowledge me. Capacity is supposed to be two thousand, not that it pulls in that many now.

Still, it's nicer than I expected, and for the next month, this place is mine.

Tonight is the start of something good. I can feel it.

"Damnation."

I jump at the female voice before a woman straightens from behind the setup of boards and sound equipment on stage.

When she spots me, her eyes narrow. "Doors don't open for another twelve hours."

"I'm not a tourist. I'm mixing tonight. Raegan Madani. Little Queen," I go on, supplying the stage name I picked years ago because of its similarity to my given name and because it gave me a persona to build on.

The woman's cropped blond hair has a little gray, but she's midthirties, slim, and wearing a green sundress. A shrewd elf with a tan. "Leni. I run the club."

"And you're American," I say, noticing the accent.

"Hawaii. Big Island, born and raised."

I take the stairs to the stage, then turn to survey the sleek, black Pioneer media players flanking the latest mixer. A lifetime of dreams turned into switches and dials that put power in one person's hands.

"It's had a makeover," she says, noticing my appreciation. "I'm taking over from the previous management long enough to get her on her feet."

"Her?"

"Every club is a woman. Don't think a man could hold this much passion or euphoria. Or this many secrets. She's had a rough patch, though." Leni pats the board but her knowing gaze lands on me. "Must sound familiar."

I bristle, hands gripping the strap on my bag tighter.

"Calling out the head of Echo Entertainment on social media for everyone to see was a dumbass move," Leni goes on.

"A woman was assaulted at their venue on a night I was playing. No one at the club or the organization took responsibility. Harrison King owns the company."

"You knew the woman who was assaulted?"

"Does it matter?"

Too many people ignore women they don't

know. I needed to look out for her, even if it was after the fact.

"Let me guess—since then, the clubs that were knocking down your door won't touch you."

I lift my bag and set it on a free spot. "This one did."

I pull out my notebook computer and peer into my bag, remembering my costumes were also in my checked bag. Shit.

"Was it worth it?" she asks.

"Yes." My gaze flicks to hers. "People need to be held responsible for their actions. I don't care how much money Harrison King has. Or how pretty he is. Or how big his dick is."

Her slow grin is feline. "You're the only one. Paparazzi stalk him. Models throw themselves at him. He built an entertainment empire most moguls on their deathbeds would envy, and he did it without a gray hair in sight."

I shiver. From sleep deprivation, not from remembering what it felt like to stand a breath away from that man.

"Rumor is he's hiding out now," Leni replies. "Maybe you hurt his feelings."

"That would require him to have feelings."

Leni smirks as she holds out a network cable. I lift the lid of my notebook and hit the power key, but the battery's dead.

"I'll never play another of his clubs for as long as I live." I pull the laptop's power cord and adapter from my bag. Before I can reach for the power bar across the desk, a smooth, impossibly male British voice comes from overhead.

"That's a shame. Because the contract you signed says that, for the next month, you're mine."

2

RAE

*H*arrison fucking King.

The man himself appears on the catwalk in one of the VIP booths, wearing tailored pants the color of sandy beaches and a white button-down shirt that skims his broad shoulders and muscled chest.

Every inch of his form screams wealth and privilege. His hair is perfectly trimmed, the dull burnished gold darkened to a warm brown in the low lights of the club.

A strong, straight nose and square jaw compete for attention with his firm lips.

He must have a decade on me but looks as if he could make the Olympic swim team without breaking a sweat.

Our first and only confrontation is forever

imprinted in my memory. When I approached the billionaire stranger at the wedding reception of two musicians who are mutual friends, I had been riding high on righteous anger. Anger I'd kept in check during the actual wedding—to spare my friends—and unleashed soon after with the help of a few drinks.

I don't make a habit of hating people, but this man makes me rethink that stance.

"What the hell is going on?" I demand.

Electric blue eyes, not unlike the neon sign outside, bore into me.

"You signed a contract to play my club."

He starts toward the stairs, taking them with leisurely strides until he reaches the main floor.

"It wasn't yours when I signed the contract." I would have noticed if his company, Echo Entertainment, had been on the documents.

"Not my problem you can't keep up with the industry."

The staff behind the bar have snapped to attention. They didn't look up when I arrived, but now, they're hustling to wipe imaginary spots off the surface while sneaking furtive looks at the man before me.

Harrison crosses to us, stopping in front of the stage. His shirt is open at the collar to expose a tan throat, the muscles flexing lightly. His mouth curves to reveal a smile as perfect as it is cold.

I whirl to face Leni, who lifts a shoulder as if anticipating my accusation.

"Listen…" she starts.

"Leni." He holds up a hand, cuts her off without so much as a word.

Arrogant prick.

I slam the cover of my notebook and slide it in my bag before shouldering it. "I'm not playing your club," I toss at the man in front of the stage. "Not tonight, not ever."

I stalk down the steps and head across the dance floor.

I make it across the club, then yank on the door.

It doesn't open.

Desperation rises up the second I feel him at my back.

"I'm disappointed." That smooth voice is inches from my ear, close enough his breath tickles my skin. "I've been anticipating this since our first meeting."

I spin around, my nostrils flaring as I stare up at his infuriatingly gorgeous face.

How could I have mistaken the man at the airport for Harrison King?

No man on earth has his intensity, his charisma.

"A woman was assaulted at my gig in LA," I bite out, angry with both of us now. "My gig at *your club*. Your booking agent didn't give a shit. No one at corporate returned my calls demanding an explanation. When I finally got to you, you didn't give a shit either."

"When you confronted me about it at a mutual friend's wedding, you mean."

He says that like it matters.

"If you think I have time to personally care for everyone who sets foot in a building with my name on the deed," he goes on, "you underestimate the size of my empire."

I lift my chin. "If you can't protect the people you serve, you have no right to one."

His throat bobs, a flicker of surprise flitting through his eyes.

Even kings have vulnerabilities.

I try the door again, realizing the lock is on. After turning it, I yank the door open, grab my bag, and run past the confused security guard on the other side.

In the parking lot, I'm breathing heavily as I pull out my phone to call Toro. I need to get out of here—out of this man's presence. At my resort, I can figure out what the hell to do next.

A ringtone sounds, but the call breaks before Toro answers.

Shit.

I scan my surroundings, my gaze landing on the busy road.

"You have an exceedingly low opinion of me," King calls from behind me as I head for the street, searching the horizon for a cab.

"I'm surprised you care what my opinion is."

His expression flickers with emotions I can't read before he slips into aristocratic arrogance once again. A resting asshole face if I ever saw one.

"I trust your attorneys looked at the terms for failure to fulfill your contractual obligations," he goes on.

The wind blows my fallen hair into my face, and I set my bag down at my feet to shove it back with vicious hands.

"Thanks to you," he drawls, "one of my top-performing venues became the worst overnight. You will recover what you cost me. For the next month, I own you. If you try to leave, I will sue you for every dollar you own. I will take your computer"—he picks up the bag at my feet, and I tense—"your music. Every scrap of clothing in your wardrobe and on your body."

Each word lands on my chest like a brick.

Breathing is hard. We're outside, but it's as if the greedy asshole has consumed all the oxygen.

"What. No response?" he chides softly.

I'm usually the type to rebel with silent resistance, but I refuse to go down without a fight. There are too many bullies in this world.

"If it takes litigation to get a woman naked..." I snatch my bag from his hands. "Your game needs work."

His mouth twists in disbelief.

Before he can respond, the horn of a car honks and a cab pulls over to the side of the road.

I reach for the back door of the car, my heart still thudding.

"If you try to leave, I will sue you for every dollar you own. I will take your computer. Your music. Every scrap of clothing in your wardrobe and on your body."

Even as the car pulls away from him, I can't kick the sickening possibility he's right.

For the next month...

The man who ruined me owns me.

3

RAE

When the cab pulls up to the sandstone villa perched halfway up a winding road and sheltered by a lush hedge of greenery, I can't help but appreciate its beauty.

Judging from the size, this villa is more like a boutique hotel than a resort. When I enter, backpack in tow, a woman looks up from where she's vacuuming. I don't spot a concierge or front desk, so I approach the woman.

"I'm supposed to be staying here tonight." I reach for my passport, but she stops me.

Her face brightens as she clasps my hand between both of hers. "*Sí, señorita.* I am Natalia." Her voice is warm and welcoming. "I will show you your room."

She leads me up a staircase and down a hall with doors on either side, half a dozen in total.

"This will meet your needs?" she asks as she opens a door.

I step into the room of pale-yellow walls, and beyond them are double doors opening to a balcony that overlooks the ocean. "It's beautiful. Thank you."

She nods before ducking out, closing the door.

The sight and the fresh scent of the water unlock my chest, a twisted knot wound tighter since my run-in with the devil himself.

I'm in another country without most of my possessions, and my only potential source of income is the man I hate.

But I know one thing—there's no way I'm playing for him. I'll walk into the sea first and never come back.

I pull out my phone, digging around to find the contract. His name's not on it anywhere, but that's not unusual for a large organization.

The amount I stand to lose by not playing has my stomach sinking.

I send the paperwork off to my lawyer anyway, asking how I can get out of it.

This gig was supposed to be my salvation. Instead, I'm being forced to play for the man I hate.

I'm used to traveling, but suddenly, I feel adrift.

I do a quick calculation of the time difference —six hours behind—before I hit a number on my phone.

"Hey!" Annie's panting voice comes through the speaker. "You caught me in the midst of my morning stomach pyrotechnics."

"Hardly seems fair Tyler's on tour and you've been hugging a toilet for the last two weeks."

My roommate from arts school and her rockstar husband are going to be parents in less than five months.

"Don't worry. He'll be making it up to me."

Her breezy tone has me shaking my head. I have no doubt she'll tell him what she wants. Or that he'll move mountains to give it to her. Their relationship is almost enough to make me believe in love.

"I was going to ask if you had a chance to lay down vocals for that track I was working on."

"I need one more listen before I send it over," she promises. "Now please distract me so I don't think about how every smell in our house makes me want to upchuck."

Her earnest plea makes my mouth twitch.

"I just got into Ibiza." I flop down on the double bed, which gives gently under my weight. The fabric smells fresh—not from-a-can fresh either. "But the residency gig isn't what I signed on for."

Telling her the full extent of what's going down might upset her or, worse, make her try to intervene.

I don't need her solving my problems. Both because I can solve them myself and because she knows what went down between Harrison and me.

We met at her wedding.

And Harrison King is a friend of her husband's.

As unlikely as it seems that the man who glowered down at me today has any friends, evidently Tyler Adams, a guy I went to school with and respect, met him on tour and they formed a genuine bond.

Annie makes a noise of sympathy. "If it's anything like doing a show on Broadway, it's exhausting and scary but rewarding too."

Doubtful.

"Where's Mr. Tall, Dark, and Broody?" I change the subject.

"Tyler's in Amsterdam this week. Since the honeymoon, I've been going into travel withdrawal. I heard Ibiza is beautiful."

My feet carry me out to the balcony. My finger trails along the sandstone half wall as I inhale the fresh air.

"Only if you're into fresh air, crystal-blue

waters, beautiful people, and partying."

She laughs. "Hard to imagine anything could ruin that. You deserve it. I don't think you've stayed in one place for a month since college."

The problem with staying in one place is you get attached to it. You expect things of the people around you.

I learned early how dangerous and destructive that can be.

"Listen," I start, "I should let you go. But it's good to hear your childish enthusiasm. You want a souvenir?"

"Bring me back a good story and we'll call it even."

I click off and stare at the water.

Harrison's right about one thing—I can't leave without a plan. Right now, if he wants to go after me legally, I have no doubt he'd win.

Annie wants a story.

I might be young, but I'm not powerless.

I won't run from this villain.

Not without getting a few swings in first.

Harrison King might be the man with the money.

But I'm the girl with the mic.

A light knock at the door has me turning back toward the room as Natalia comes in, a perplexed look on her face. "Where are your bags?"

"The airline lost them."

Her eyes widen. "*Dios mío*. I can take you shopping, if you like, or send you to the best boutiques."

I cross to the middle of the room and look down at my clothes. I need something to wear tonight if I'm not leaving today. "Maybe not the best boutiques," I warn because that sounds expensive. "If I called them and told them what I wanted, could they send a few items over?"

"Of course."

"Including a wig," I say, setting my phone on the dresser and tugging out the half-assed bun I made on the side of the road an hour ago. "Blond," I decide.

If it's a strange request, she doesn't balk. "You should go to the beach. We also have a pool and a jacuzzi. Enjoy yourself before you have to work. You're too young to look so serious."

Inspired, I reach for my computer.

Natalia is right. Just because I'm here doesn't mean I can't enjoy myself a little.

Defiance flows through my veins as I send off a quick text to Annie with some lyrics for a new verse.

My contract says I'll play for Harrison King.

It doesn't say I have to do it nicely.

4

HARRISON

"We're here, *señor*." My driver's eyes meet mine in the rearview mirror as he pulls up in front of the club.

I straighten my suit. "Thank you, Toro."

"Are you sure you're ready?"

I frown. "It's a Thursday night like any Thursday night."

Except it doesn't feel like it. My body is humming, braced for a fight or coming off of one.

I shift out before Toro can open my door. He follows me around anyway, stubbornly taking the car door in his aging hands as I fasten my jacket.

"It's a new club. The renovations are only just complete. And new talent," he goes on as I start for the entrance.

I pull up, turning to cock my head at him. He only nods before retreating to the driver's side.

New talent indeed.

I head to the back door. Security stands at attention when they see me.

A man with a purpose is dangerous to the world.

A man without a purpose is dangerous to himself.

When I enter a room, it's to tell people what I want and make it immediately clear I'm going to get it. The faster they see that, the more painless it is.

My first acquisition was filthy and spare, cobbled together like the money I used to finance it. Now, I stride down a private hallway used for deliveries and talent, absorbing the fresh paint and shining floors with a grim satisfaction.

When I bought Debajo, everything was in disrepair, as if its name meant not only "beneath" but "forgotten."

It takes a particular eye to see what others miss. But for a man who looks beneath the surface, one who's as relentless as he is patient...

There is treasure to be found.

Now, the club is a cool kiss. An elegant reminder of how far I've come.

I wish my parents could see it.

The twinge in my gut sneaks up on me, lingering like the burn of bad whisky.

A budding actress who's rising to stardom makes her way toward me, coming from the direction of the club.

"Hello, gorgeous," she purrs, the telltale enthusiasm of alcohol lingering in her voice as she stops in my path with an inviting smile. "Haven't seen you stateside for way too long."

"You came to find me and enjoy my hospitality," I reply evenly. "So, my plan worked."

She slips her hand inside my shirt, and I smoothly withdraw it, my grip firm enough there's disappointment in her eyes.

A hundred men in this place would take her home tonight.

I'm not one of them.

I used to enjoy beautiful women, particularly ones who made a lifestyle of *being* enjoyed.

No more.

Not since I let myself believe one could stand at my side and be what I needed. Trusting a woman with my life, my home, my future, cost me far more than the years I invested in that relationship.

It won't happen again.

I straighten my shirt before I continue down the hall, making eye contact with the security guard at the end and nodding to him to keep an eye on her and make sure she doesn't find trouble.

I feel the pulsing music through the leather of my dress shoes before I hear it. I approach the door that leads to the club, then turn and take the stairs up to the second level. At the top, security opens the door. Pulsing music flows into me, through me.

The metal grate flooring creaks beneath my feet on my way to my private booth next to two other VIP booths upstairs. Below, revelers drink and dance to the opening act.

I pause, one storey up with a perfect view of the performers and the crowd.

I've been out all day but have confirmed with Natalia and Toro that my newest contractor intends to play tonight.

I knew she would see reason. She might be fiery, but there was no way she'd abandon this. I'd sue her fast enough she'd land on that curvy bottom.

The first time we met, at the island wedding of my friend Tyler, she was fury itself. Barely waiting until after the cake had been cut and the couple rode off into shining bliss to rain righteous hellfire on me.

I told her the same thing I'd tell anyone criticizing my business:

Thank you very fucking little for your input.

Evidently, she wasn't pleased with my reaction.

A single social media post condemning my business caused the door income of my best club to drop by half overnight and spurred a bloody mountain of paperwork and hostile media inquiries my team had to deal with. Most of them made their way up to me and ruined a string of otherwise good days.

A small consolation was that she exploded in an equally destructive way.

My PR staff told me that while a few fans had applauded the move, many were ambivalent. More importantly, no club owner from London to Miami would touch her for fear she'd find fault with their operations.

Part of me envies her idealism. We were all naïve once, even if the last time I knew so little of the world I was still in knee socks.

"Whisky, Mr. King?" the upstairs VIP bartender asks, and I nod.

"In my booth."

"Sí, señor. You have a visitor."

Before I can demand who the fuck is in my private space, the bartender's gone. I round the corner of my booth and stiffen.

"Let me guess—half your renovation budget was for the club and half for whisky." The last person I'd expect is sitting in the booth in khakis and a polo shirt, nursing a drink.

"Ash. I didn't realize you were coming."

My brother Sebastian is a decade younger, and has a propensity to avoid me unless he wants to lay blame at my feet.

"Premier League has been over for a week." He flashes a grin. "Thought I'd raid the bar at your newest club."

"I've bought two more since."

"Yet you're still here. If I didn't know better, I'd say you were hiding."

Ash doesn't miss a thing. He's the smarter of the two of us, yet he plays professional football and I'm the one running a corporation.

"I'm not hiding. I'm relaxing."

His smirking gaze runs from my dress shoes up the suit to my tight face.

"You look positively rejuvenated," he quips. "When will you stop this relentless quest for acquisitions? When you own every entertainment venue in the world?"

I accept the thirty-year-old Glen Scotia whisky the bartender brings on a monogrammed napkin. "We'll find out."

"Our parents wouldn't want you to do this," he says.

My grip on the glass tightens. "You don't know what they'd want. You were a boy when they died."

My brother shifts out of his seat. He has the same hair and eyes as me, but he's a few inches shorter. He's made the most of what he's been given and is now a forward for the second-best professional football club in England since getting drafted out of uni last year.

"I thought you'd started to mellow when you were with *her*." My brother leans over the railing next to me. "You stepped back from the business. Started genuinely enjoying life a little. It was good to see, Harry."

I sip, and the smooth alcohol lingers on my taste buds. "Love is an illusion. I was a fool to think it was more."

The tabloids paint me as a richer-than-Midas entertainment mogul with no greater pleasure than adding to the piles of money I've made.

It's easier for me that they do.

Their needling over superficial flaws and supposed weaknesses doesn't bother me.

It keeps them from digging at the real ones.

The crowd below us is dancing, losing themselves in the music pounding through the speakers, reverberating off every wall.

"Leni texted this afternoon to say I should come down to see a show," Ash says over the music. "She also said a woman tore you a new one." His grin flashes white for a second before the club lights go dark.

The hairs on my neck lift in anticipation.

The DJs change over. It happens every night between the opening act and the headliner, but tonight, I feel it.

It's a tug in my gut, a thrumming in my veins.

It's why I came, though I'd never admit it.

The way she spoke to me earlier... No one challenges me like that.

She can't honestly think she'll get out of this deal. The fact that she's here means she's admitted the truth.

She'll bend to me, like everyone else does.

When the black light comes on, the crowd erupts.

She's on stage, her hair, trousers, and cropped body-hugging top glowing white before the lights change to a more normal range.

Out of costume, off stage, she's moody, seething. A girl who hissed at me like a cornered animal.

On it, she's vibrant.

Her clothes cling to her body in a way that draws attention to her curves but also lets her move uninhibited. A long, blond wig is a stark contrast to her warm skin and dark lashes, thick and lowered as she studies the computer in front of her with the intensity of a rocket scientist navigating a launch.

"Little Queen," Ash observes. "The name suits her."

I've always preferred women as careless as they are beautiful. But there's something about her that makes it impossible to look away.

"She owes me," I say at last, my voice gravel. "And even queens must pay their debts."

This arrangement is supposed to be strictly business, but the idea of seeing her admit she can't fight me is oddly appealing.

Fuck. I need to get laid if a naïve young American hurling insults at my decency and my empire makes my cock hard.

But I'm still watching her, trapped in the limbo she creates with her energy, her music, leaning in like a shameless voyeur.

She's the rebel girl every horny teenage boy at boarding school badmouthed, then secretly fucked his hand to at night while wishing it was her pussy instead.

I expect my brother to rip into me for being soulless. When I finally force my attention to him, he's watching her, as entranced as every one of the drunk and high patrons below.

"She's pretty."

Alarm coils in my gut. Before I can snap a response, or even decipher the layers of my reaction, the track changes.

Boys want a fight
Want to prove they're right
Let them scratch and hiss
Circle when they piss—
The words seep into my skin.

My gaze narrows on the DJ, and as if she senses it, she looks up toward our booth.

And in a move as graceful as it is deliberate, she flips both middle fingers.

Ash barks out a laugh, the genuine kind I haven't heard in far too long. "Fuck, Harry. I think I'm in love."

5

RAE

"Hello, American," a male voice whisper-shouts as I yank off my headphones at the end of my set.

The man standing within earshot is my age and the kind of preppy handsome that sells Ralph Lauren campaigns.

I look at the security guard, who is facing the other way. *Not again.*

"Hey!" I shout at the guard, who finally turns back, spotting the man next to me.

"He's a VIP," the guard mouths.

Perfect. I should've known Debajo would be one of those places where VIPs get whatever they want.

"Don't worry. We're going to be friends." The man who approached me offers a blinding grin that's familiar and not. "That was quite the set. Have a drink with me."

"I'm not sticking around."

"Please?"

I could use a drink. Plus, I won't be able to sleep for hours.

With luck, I'll get to bed by six o'clock in the morning, stare at the ceiling for a few hours while waiting for a response from my lawyer, then drag myself out of bed midafternoon to do a little sightseeing and get my bag before catching a flight out of here.

"You're buying," I inform him.

Before heading to the bar, I stop in the bathroom, pop two ibuprofen, and wipe the sweat from my face and neck.

My new friend meets me outside. "Not going to lose this wig?"

I hold a strand up. "This is my natural hair color."

He grins. "I'm Ash. Now is when you tell me your real name."

"I don't think so." I settle in next to him as we head through the private backstage halls. Security lets us pass without comment.

"Damn it. It was going to seem natural when I called you Raegan, but I guess I can't say you told me."

I stop abruptly. "How did you—"

"Come on, blondie." He grabs my wrist and tugs me after him.

My real name might be on every contract, but I keep my personal life separate where I can. It's strange hearing not only my nickname, which all my friends use, but my full name.

"Wish I could hide out for privacy," he says, reading my mind. "I play pro football."

I scan his lean form. "Quarterback?"

He scoffs. "Proper football."

He holds the door for me, and I walk through into another world. There's a private bar, beautiful people lounging at tables, a poker game in one corner. The veneer of casual exclusivity is impossible to miss. Diamonds against crushed velvet. Wool suiting on faded leather stools.

My gaze lands on the table of men playing cards. One in particular has me stiffening.

Harrison King is wearing a suit tonight. He's impeccable. Not runway-model beautiful, but mafia-don ruthless. Sharp angles and unyielding planes. His strong face is sculpted into an intense study of the cards in front of him, the ones on the table.

Ash follows my gaze and snorts. "Don't let him ruin your fun. Just because he's a prick and he owns the place..."

I arch a brow. "I'm glad I'm not the only one who thinks so."

We head for the bar, and he orders me a cocktail.

"Harrison King stole my belongings," Ash goes on after. "Held my head underwater until I conceded. Told on me." There's a pause as I process each of these transgressions. Finally, Ash raises his glass, grinning. "He's my older brother."

"So, he sent you to make nice." I shouldn't be talking to anyone who shares an ounce of DNA with the man I loathe.

"Hardly. He'll be upset I'm talking to you."

I take a sip. The vodka soda is clean on my tongue, in my throat, as music from the afterparty outside drifts in.

"Then by all means, continue."

Ash barks out a laugh, blue eyes warmer than his brother's. "If you hate him, why are you playing his club?"

"A mistake. One I'm going to fix in the morning so I can get out of here."

"That's unfortunate. You should stay."

"Help the man I hate make money?" I scoff.

"I'm going to tell you a secret. You're making money too, Raegan."

"Rae," I correct, not because we're friends but

because hearing my full name weirds me out. "Why do you care?"

He turns the glass in his hands. "Women have followed him willingly all his life. I think you'd show him there's another way."

"He wouldn't appreciate another way. The man treats women like disposable napkins."

"He proposed to the last woman he dated. They were engaged, until she ended it."

I cut Ash a surprised look. The idea of Harrison King having a softer side, of wanting to spend his life with another person, is hard to picture.

"I can't imagine what he did to deserve to get dumped." I don't hide the sarcasm, but I'm still processing the "engaged" part.

"He trusted her too much." My new companion's voice softens. "We date the people we think we deserve. Though he'd never admit it, my brother doesn't think he's worthy of better."

My attention drags across the room to the man in question, hating that those words make me question Harrison King's spot in hell.

I realize my mistake too late, because he's spotted me.

Harrison King rises from the table with the grace of a shadow. Now, he's headed this way.

I can't help comparing the two men. Their

coloring is similar, a faint tan from the sun under dirty-blond hair. The same magnetic blue eyes. But where Ash's friendly, Harrison is cold. Cut from marble.

"Brother," Ash greets him as he arrives. "You're the only person in a suit at this hour." He nods to the rest of the room, where every other man has long since stripped his jacket off.

"I wear one because it's my club," Harrison replies.

I take a drink. "There are other options to hide the stick up your ass besides Hugo Boss."

"It's Brioni."

Ash cackles in delight. "I was telling our little queen how exceptional she was tonight."

"When my club is full, I'll praise her," Harrison states.

Ash turns back to greet a friend, leaving me and Harrison at the bar.

"Unfortunately, this was a one-night-only performance." I shift off the stool. "But I'm glad you enjoyed it."

"Not half as much as you did." He blocks my path. "I saw the way you lose yourself up there. In *my club*, which you seem intent on despising."

My body tingles, from his closeness and the intimacy of his words.

"It's a persona. Not me."

"You can't hide how it makes you feel. You've had orgasms less satisfying than what you experienced tonight."

Anyone in the crowd could tell I was having a good time. But the way this man watched me, the way he's watching me now, feels as if he sees under my clothes.

Under my skin.

The thrumming in my stomach streaks lower, between my thighs.

Laughter goes up from across the room, but I can't look away from Harrison King.

"You know nothing about my orgasms, and you never will."

I'm hot, and I pull the hair over one shoulder to leave the other bare. He follows the movement, attention lingering on my exposed skin and heating it like a filthy kiss.

"You told Leni this afternoon that you hated me no matter how pretty I was or how big my cock is, which means you've considered both."

My breath catches.

"That's why you're angry," he continues. "You hate me, but the thought of me gets you off. I might be a villain, but in your dreams I still slink into your room at night and make you come."

His voice strokes down my spine like a filthy

whisper. That decadent accent he deploys like a weapon is obscene.

"The only thing I've thought about," I say, nodding to his belt, "is how you must be compensating for something to be this much of an asshole."

When my attention drags back up to his face, the expression scorches me alive.

A cheer goes up from behind us, and we turn to see Leni come in the door, lifting her hands. "You were great," she informs me with a grin, offering a high five. "See you back here Monday?" She looks between Harrison and me. "Unless the boss eats you first."

The man at my side growls, and Leni laughs.

I'm mystified by the dynamic, still remembering the way he shut her up without a word earlier.

When I reach for my phone, Harrison frowns.

"What are you doing?"

"Calling Toro for a ride."

"He's an old man who needs his sleep." He jerks his head at one of the bartenders, who reaches for a house phone on the wall. "A car will be here in five minutes."

He gestures toward the hallway, then follows me out.

The man is a ruthless billionaire. Incapable of compromise. Incapable of love.

Except he might be a villain to me, but he's not to Leni. To Toro. To his brother.

I have a handful of friends now, but a network of people I go back with? People I trust and who trust me?

That sounds like make believe.

Security holds the outside door for us, the guard already nodding to me with familiarity. "Mr. King. Miss... Queen."

A half laugh is out of my lips before I step out into the cool evening. Harrison cocks his head.

"Cute couple," I drawl.

I catch his eye over my shoulder, and he huffs out a breath when he realizes I'm trying to piss him off.

"You're the one making this hard."

I rub my hands over my skin in response to the sudden chill—of the night air or his words. "Hard's the only way I know."

He strips off his jacket, and my gaze is drawn to the muscles of his shoulders and chest through the shirt beneath.

I'm distracted enough it takes me a moment to realize his intention as he closes the distance between us.

"No. Don't—"

I lift both hands defensively, but he drapes the expensive fabric around my shoulders and pulls the lapels closed over my chest before I can stop him.

"You'd probably like to freeze to death your first night." His closeness invades my senses, makes it hard to think. "If only to leave me in a jam."

"I told you, I'm leaving in the morning."

I start to shrug out of the coat, but he stops me.

"Keep it."

What kind of a man is fastidious enough to wear designer suits but doesn't care about giving one away to spare me a few moments' chill? Before I find a good answer, the cab pulls up.

As I drive away from Harrison King for the second time today, I finger the edge of the jacket.

I'm alone again.

The rush of relief I expected doesn't come.

6

RAE

"Have you found my bag?" I press a hand to my face to stifle the yawn. It's noon, and I managed two hours of fitful sleep in the luxurious bed at the villa.

"Unfortunately not." The woman at the airline repeats the words I heard yesterday about reimbursement as I flop onto the bed and drop the phone next to me.

I stare longingly at the bedside table, where my bottle of pills would typically be. Instead of my belongings, the only way I've personalized this room is by throwing Harrison's suit jacket over the lampshade until I can figure out what to do with it.

After, I make a call to my attorney, who says there's no clear loophole to get me out of this contract and avoid the damages written in—which I never thought I'd be in a position to consider.

I'm stranded in Ibiza without options, my pills... even a damned razor.

The jet lag is messing with my head.

My workout clothes were in my checked bag, so I pull on my sneakers and the skinny jeans from yesterday.

One glance in the mirror over the dresser shows my hair is a mess of craziness. I yank it all up into a ponytail before I peer out into the hall. No sign of anyone.

When I reach the top of the stairs, rapid shouting in Spanish comes from below, ending with, "Get back here!"

Then I'm attacked.

A big, black dog with brown eyes barrels toward me, leaping. His paws hit my thighs, his lolling tongue licking at my arms.

I catch him awkwardly.

"My apologies, señorita. He loves people," Natalia calls up the stairs from the doorway of the kitchen.

The creature lets me set his paws back on the ground but continues to eye me as if I'm the only thing he's wanted his whole life.

"His master hasn't had time to take him out for

his walk today. I was late finishing my errands yesterday, and..."

Probably because she went to get me clothes.

"Are you going for a walk? Would you take him? He's no trouble."

Guilt has me saying, "Ah, sure."

We never had pets growing up. My parents are both in tech—my dad left Tehran for computer engineering at UCLA. They've always kept long hours, and though their careers meant my brothers and I never suffered materially, a dog would've been one too many interruptions for their goals.

I take the stairs down as Natalia gets the dog's leash and fastens it on, meeting me at the front door with a grateful smile.

"You would like breakfast when you return?" Natalia gestures toward the kitchen. "And tea?"

I'm not used to being served by anyone, but my stomach growls—probably because I haven't eaten in almost twenty-four hours. "Coffee would be great."

I take the dog out and let the sea breeze go to work on my brain.

Telemanco, where the villa is, isn't as busy as Ibiza Town. It's relaxed and stunning, and I could totally take a vacation here if I had the money.

As I walk, I use my phone to read articles about

Harrison King and Echo Entertainment. Search engines keep insisting I want to know about his travels with his ex-fiancée, model Eva Nilsson. There are photos of them in cafés, on the red carpet, at charity galas, and even on the beach.

She's stunning, and I can't help noticing the way she beams at him.

Maybe Ash is full of shit. I don't see a woman who would've left. She looks utterly devoted.

Not that there's *nothing* to respect about Harrison King. He relentlessly built an entertainment empire, so he's clearly focused. But he's soulless.

It was easy to forget when those bottomless blue eyes were boring into me last night in the VIP room. For a moment, I couldn't help wondering how deep you'd have to fall to find something more in him, and whether it might be worth it.

A grinning old man descends on us, speaking to the dog. "His name?" he asks me after a moment.

I tuck the phone away, stalling. "Licorice."

The man looks surprised, but the dog barks agreeably. After a few more pets, we continue on our way.

"That was embarrassing," I inform the dog.

He cocks his head, lifting both ears.

After we're interrupted another few times, I

realize walking the dog is not a way to get quiet time to myself.

So, I make a game of it and give him a new name every time.

"Costas."

"Siegfried."

"Roy."

I wind "Bowie's" leash tighter to rein him in as I scroll through my banking information on my phone.

I don't check it often because the only thing I need money for is a roof over my head and plane tickets from show to show, both of which are usually covered by the venue.

Still, the balance is lower than I'd like.

I scan through the recent transactions.

One automatic withdrawal from last month—rapidly approaching for this month—makes me curse.

I hit a contact on my phone, chewing my lip as I wait for the line to pick up.

"Hello, cousin," I say when it does.

"Hey." Rustling sounds come over the line as if Callie's getting out of bed.

Since we were kids, we had a running joke of greeting each other formally. Living a few hours apart, we'd mostly see one another at family events and holidays. We weren't allowed to have cellphones until high school, and we weren't supposed to use our computers to message.

Of course, we did anyway, but we kept up appearances to fool our parents.

Since high school, I haven't been close with my brothers or parents. Callie's the nearest thing I have to family, and though we don't hang out on the regular, she's the one person who's stood by me since I was a kid when I needed it.

I picture her in the West LA apartment she shares with a roommate as I press the phone to my ear to pick up more sounds around her, clues as to her well-being. "Are you working this week?"

"Um, I'm not sure." More noises, as if she's moving around.

My cousin is normally upbeat and inquisitive. Her response makes me pull up, stepping away from the route so we don't get trampled by runners or tourists. "Listen. I'm calling because I might not have the money this month."

I hold my breath as I wait for her disappointment, or protest.

"It's fine," she says, her voice flat.

"You don't need it?"

"We need way more. Something we were counting on fell through. I'm not sure we'll make it this time."

Alarm has my hand tightening on the phone. "How much are you short?"

She sighs. "Twenty thousand."

Shit.

There's no way I have that kind of free cash, even *with* this contract.

"Can you get a loan?"

"I tried. We've just been served an eviction notice."

The sunshine is every bit as bright, but as the dog tugs me down the path, my feet are heavy as bricks.

"Your landlord can't kick you out, especially given the circumstances."

"He doesn't care. I'm going to be spending the next week packing."

I've been trying to figure out how to leave Ibiza in one piece, but my chest aches when I think of Callie, the one person who's always had my back.

When I help her, it's because I want to and I can. Not because she asks.

"Don't pack yet. Let me get back to you."

When I return to the villa, I'm still trying to think of how to help Callie.

I step inside, the leash looped around my wrist. I stop to yank off a shoe.

Before I can, the dog bolts.

I trip each step as he drags me across the floor, up the stairs.

"Stop. Licorice! Costas! Siegfried! Roy! Bowie!"

He hesitates at the last word, and I manage to suck in a breath before he lunges again, nearly knocking me flat on my face.

He galumphs down the hall with me stumbling behind. The door at the end is cracked, and he sticks his nose in before shoving it wide and barreling into the room.

I barely notice the wood furniture and sunny orange walls of an office.

Especially when my gaze lands on the man on the phone, seated on the edge of the desk.

"Unacceptable. We had this solved last week." Harrison King is impeccable in dress slacks and a blue shirt that matches his eyes. Eyes that widen when the dog launches himself onto the man.

"That was the whole point of the deal," he bites out into the phone. "We invested in the renovations expecting a return. This is a multibillion-dollar business, not fucking child's play."

I stop in the middle of the room, the leash still taut.

"That's your job," he goes on. "I suggest you do

it." Harrison stabs a finger at his phone, ending the call.

"Down, Bowie," I say belatedly. I don't know what Harrison King is doing here, but seeing the dog put his paws all over the expensive clothes is oddly satisfying.

Harrison's gaze drags up my body from my running shoes, a slow study. Judging from his drawn brows, it seems to leave him with no more answers than when he started.

"Bowie?" He shifts off the desk and crosses to me.

"I don't know his name. But he seems pretty rock and roll."

Harrison loosens the leash from around my wrist. The Rolex on his wrist glints in the light from the open windows.

"It's Barney," he says as he releases me. "And he's my dog."

Surprise slams into me.

"You and your dog are staying at my villa." I look around the office again, needing somewhere to focus that's not his unrelenting attention.

"No. You and your attitude are staying at *my* villa."

Horror washes over me.

I slept at this man's house last night? Walked his damned dog?

What kind of a controlling freak invites a contractor who hates him to live with him?

And skips the invitation, I might add.

"Why?" I blurt.

His gaze is chastising. "I decided it would be easier to keep an eye on you and ensure you complied with your contractual responsibilities. An impulsive decision I'm already regretting," he adds, frowning as he searches my face.

I could scream, but my attention drags back to his watch. I could probably pawn the thing and solve all of my cousin's financial problems.

Harrison King could snap his fingers and pay off the debt of a small country.

My mind spins as I concoct a plan that keeps me one step ahead. "About the contract—"

"I've told you, if you break the contract, I'll sue you."

"I want to renegotiate."

His mouth snaps shut.

"You've invested a lot in Debajo's renovations. Give me twenty-five percent of the door for the next month and I'll fill it."

He folds his arms across his chest, the blue fabric pulling across firm muscles. The way his eyes narrow as he clicks smoothly into business mode is as compelling as it is intimidating. "Because you can do things my PR firm can't?"

I match his posture. "Obviously."

I'm bluffing. Publicity isn't my strong suit, unless you count publicly going down in flames. But he doesn't need to know that.

"And if you don't?"

"I don't get paid. But when you make money, I make money."

Something nudges at my thigh, and I look down to see Barney inserting himself between us, tail wagging.

"Ten percent," Harrison replies as I bend down to scratch the dog's head.

"Twenty. And I'm moving to alternative accommodations."

"Fifteen, you stay, plus I get three requests of my choosing."

The evenness of his voice has my jaw dropping. This man acts as if he always gets his way.

"What kind of requests?"

"Any requests," he says impatiently. "If I want you to clean the pool using your thong as a filter, you will."

My hands fist at my sides. "I'm not a genie in a fucking bottle. Clean your own pool."

Harrison turns away. "Then there's no deal."

The dismissal is swift and brutal.

I don't understand his endgame. One more

mystery about the already-confusing man before me.

But I know that what he wants is to put me in a corner.

"These requests don't involve other people," I say at last, and his head cocks.

"Only you."

The way he says those two words makes me shiver.

"Eighteen, plus your stupid requests," I counter.

His blue gaze is intense enough I feel my ribs crack.

We shake, and electricity runs up my arm at his touch.

He pulls away first. "I'll have my solicitor send a new copy of the contract. I expect your signature by the end of the day. Along with my jacket."

My head snaps up to meet his mocking expression. "You knew you'd get it back. That's why you gave it to me."

"It's Brioni." He says it as if it's an answer.

"You're unbelievable. Controlling, demanding, manipulative... No wonder your fiancée left you."

His fist clenches around the leash, and when he speaks, his voice is dangerously low. "Be careful what you say when you still want things from me."

A knock on the door is followed by the housekeeper's immediate entrance.

"Ah, *perdón!*" she gushes when she sees us. "I see you and Señor King are getting more acquainted." She's either oblivious to the tension or ignores it. "I thought señorita would like to know her suitcase is in her room."

My heart leaps. "The airline found it?"

"No," Harrison intervenes. "The contents were spilled when we retrieved them, but I trust everything is there."

He found my suitcase when the airline couldn't. Through what, some kind of billionaire black magic?

Relief surges through me, though it's short-lived when I remind myself who's responsible for it.

His voice follows me to the door. "You may buy replacements for anything missing from your luggage and charge them to my account, with one exception. I do not tolerate my employees on drugs of any kind."

Son of a...

"And don't forget my jacket."

I sprint down the hall and unzip my suitcase, tossing clothes and wigs and toiletries out onto the floor.

The pill bottle is zipped into an inside pocket.

And it's empty.

7

HARRISON

My father used to say, "You can't control a man's thoughts, but you can command his actions."

That's what I'm intent on doing today in the office—forcing men's hands.

One man's hand in particular.

On paper, Christian Geroux owns Ibiza's greatest club.

In my mind, it's already mine.

I've wanted it since I was twenty-one.

Finally, I got word he's open to selling. I won't waste this chance.

But making headway amassing the greatest collection of entertainment venues in the world requires the right frame of mind.

I finish my outdoor workout before seven,

ready to take on the day and already thinking about my meetings and strategies for my next acquisition.

I'm not thinking about the young woman I installed in my villa.

At the time, it seemed like a way to supervise her. I regretted the decision the moment she tripped into my office uninvited yesterday, towed by my dog like a water skier behind a furry yacht.

After acting as if she'd have cut off a limb if it would have gotten her out of the contract she'd signed, she flipped my deal and proposed a new one.

Negotiation 101. When you have all the leverage, there's no need to make further concessions.

But she caught me off guard, and I was curious what had changed for her since the night before when I'd set her in a cab with my favorite jacket around her shoulders.

The one I found swimming in my pool the next afternoon, the chlorine doing God knows what to the wool and the striped lining.

I ground my teeth together as I retrieved it with a cleaning implement, looking up to be sure she wasn't watching from her balcony.

Clean your own pool, she'd said.

She's nothing like the women I spend time

with. She says she doesn't care for money or wealth.

Except she asked for a raise.

Which means, on one level, she's exactly like the women I spend time with.

Now, when I return to the villa after my work-out, there's a sweater hanging on the back of a chair at the dining table.

My first thought is of payback. Dropping this into the pool and picturing her finding it there.

What the fuck is she doing to me?

I'm thirty-five years old, and I'm giddy with the prospect of ruining something of hers just to see her reaction.

The fabric is surprisingly soft as I lift it. A thin woven cover-up that's more feminine than I expect.

"What are you doing?" Natalia's voice makes my spine stiffen like a schoolboy caught masturbating.

I glance back to see her watching from the kitchen. I lower the garment, trying to forget the scent, warm and floral with something like vanilla beneath.

"Removing this from my dining room."

I start up the stairs to the open hallway that runs along one side of the villa, her sweater dangling from my fingertips like a limp rag.

Now, Rae's door is closed—it's midafternoon, and she's still asleep despite not having a show last night—but sounds inside have me frowning. Movement, shuffling.

Is someone else in there?

The possibility arouses dark thoughts.

First, she destroys my jacket. Then brings someone home to my house...

I crack the door, and my dog comes barreling out.

Light beyond the door beckons, and I peer inside.

She's alone in bed.

On her side facing the door, her dark hair is a wild mane around her head.

Her baggy T-shirt is twisted, pulling tight across her breasts, as if she was fighting sleep itself. Her lips are parted, her lashes a thick fringe that twitches against her cheeks as she dreams.

A rope tugs tight low in my gut.

Is there any time of day, alone or surrounded by people, when she finds peace?

I fold the sweatshirt and lay it on the dresser, taking in the belongings scattered around the room. My fingers itch to straighten the clothes and gadgets I went through myself when the bag arrived thanks to a call placed by one of my staff to the airline.

Denim. Off-label trainers. Cotton lingerie.

The wigs are curious. She owns as many of those as clothes, yet most women I know spend hours and thousands of dollars to try to replicate what her hair seems to do naturally.

There's no sign of the unlabelled pill bottle I found in her bag.

It had to have been recreational. No seasoned traveler would pack a necessary medication in her checked bag and risk losing it with a missing suitcase.

Drug use in Ibiza is practically a prerequisite, and I can't keep it out of my clubs. But I can keep it out of my employees, which was why I dumped the pills without a second thought.

Rae stirs, mumbling under her breath.

"What was that?" I murmur.

She repeats the single word, still sound asleep.

Adrenaline and dark triumph chase through my veins.

If she was mine, I'd shift over her on the bed, brush the hair from her face, and wake her slowly. The brush of a knuckle along the softness of her cheek. The press of my body against the curves of hers, enough to have her responding in kind even in sleep.

But she's not mine.

I won't claim another woman as mine again. I

might take them to bed—not that even that idea has held much appeal recently—but I won't offer them my life, my heart.

Because those things aren't what they truly want and because they're nothing I can offer again.

She's here to fill my club and repay her debt.

I slip out of her room before she wakes.

The morning passes in a frustrating glut. The new initiatives at my clubs are taking time and money, and I'm being reminded what a headache acquisitions are as the man standing between me and my latest prize refuses to give a straight answer to my offer.

The club I'm seeking to add to Echo Entertainment isn't only a line item on a balance sheet.

It's personal.

Since my split with Eva, the tabloids accuse me of hiding out in my Ibiza villa.

I let them.

Perhaps there's been some self pity, but I'm laying the groundwork for the biggest deal of my life. I'm in control of a multibillion-dollar company, not a fool nursing a broken heart.

From this day on, every ounce of my attention,

my money, and my influence will be devoted to winning La Mer.

When I jog down the stairs for lunch, the sight at the bottom has me swallowing an irritated groan.

The sweatshirt is back on the kitchen table as if I never took it upstairs.

I watch Rae from behind as she makes coffee, moving easily around my kitchen in faded jeans and an orange T-shirt that has slipped off one shoulder. Her hair is caught in a thick ponytail that lays over the opposite shoulder and has me remembering how wild it looked earlier as she talks on the phone and rubs her neck.

"When can I speak with him?" She takes a sip from her mug, then makes a sound of displeasure. "I'm sure he's up to his ass in requests, but have him call me."

She hangs up, tucking the phone in the back pocket of her tight jeans.

"Boyfriend dodging you?" My slow drawl has the intended effect of scaring the ever-loving fuck out of her as she whirls to face me.

Most women find me appealing, but she seems to decide I'm barely worth sharing the kitchen with when she points at her mug. "Instant coffee should be banned. I pegged you as a sadist, not a masochist."

She turns her back on me before I can respond, rubbing her temples before sliding one hand down to her neck.

Withdrawal symptoms. My sympathy fades.

"I meant what I said about staying clean while you're in my employ." The sharpness in my tone makes Rae stiffen.

"Well, now that you've tossed my stash, I guess I'll have to. What exactly did that look like to you? E? Cocaine? GHB?"

"The newest craze is 2CB—"

"Is that what was in my bag?"

My gaze narrows. "I don't know."

"It's a headache. Not withdrawal." She nods toward her notebook computer on the kitchen table before dumping the contents of her mug into the sink. "Been bent over that for twelve-plus-hour days since I was a teenager."

"So, what, two years, then?"

The comment earns me side-eye as she puts a kettle on and fixes something else on the counter obscured behind her body. "I'm twenty-four. I've been doing this ten years."

I cross to her and press a thumb into the muscle where her shoulder joins her neck inside the wide strap of her bra, and she sucks in a breath. "What are you doing?"

Rae tries to twist away, but I don't let her. "It's a

trigger point. Breathe."

"You are a sadist."

"Give me thirty seconds. If it's not better, you can call me whatever you want."

For once, she does what I say.

The muscle starts to give under my hands, and I rub a small, deliberate circle that makes her hiss.

I let my curiosity get the better of me. "So, you started at fourteen. High school dropout?"

"Got my GED at sixteen and finished early so I could work on music."

Determined.

"Plus, I don't sleep much."

I switch to the other side of her neck and dig in there. This time, she doesn't jerk away.

"You looked as if you were sleeping fine this morning."

She rips herself out of my hands, bracing against the sink and turning to level me with accusing eyes. "You were in my room?!"

"I returned your sweater. You're lucky it suffered a kinder fate than my jacket."

"And you stuck around to watch me."

"You talk in your sleep. Not my fault you were saying my name."

I'm expecting her to snap back at me, maybe even hit me, but her expression is shocked.

"I didn't." The whisper drags along my skin,

and fuck if I can't help thinking how she'd sound whispering other things.

"You did," I promise.

Her throat works as she swallows.

A timer goes off, and she slips out from where I have her against the sink.

The knee-jerk disappointment makes me grimace.

I have no interest in her, not as a woman. But the rejection is still painful.

I turn to find her pouring coffee into a mug. She holds it out. "Real coffee. I bought it in town."

"There isn't real or fake coffee..." I take a sip, the flavors mingling pleasantly in my mouth.

Rae's face lights with triumph, her lips curving. "I told you."

Ash was right. She is really fucking pretty.

Especially when she smiles.

It's the first time she's beamed in my direction, because I would've remembered.

And it's a good thing. If her negotiation had opened with that, she might own my villa right now.

My chest warms, my cold heart thudding harder against my ribs.

"La Mer," she goes on, oblivious to my turmoil. "It's bigger than Coachella, than Vegas, than anywhere. Why don't you own it?"

"I'm working on it. The things most worth having take time to acquire."

She reaches for the mug, and our fingers brush.

I wanted to catch her off guard, but it's me who's rocked when the bolt of attraction has my abs clenching under my dress shirt.

Her eyes widen before she pulls away and heads for the dining table.

"So, how are you going to fill my club?" I ask as she drops into the chair.

I grab the wrapped sandwich Natalia made me knowing I'd come for it when I was ready before returning to perch on the edge of the table.

"I have to give them a different experience every time. Plus, I'm figuring out how to get on the right people's radar."

"Debajo isn't going to be the 'it' place," she goes on. "It's a basement. The place for those who don't want to go to the 'it' place."

"People like you? The rebels and outcasts?"

"I'll take that as a compliment."

"You should."

Her gaze flicks to mine, surprised.

"You're abrasive and petulant." I can't help going on. "But add a wig, a hundred thousand euros of sound equipment, and some strobe lights? A rebel girl can turn into a nightclub goddess."

Her lips part. "Goddess."

"I'm not referring to your looks," I say evenly, though the more I stare at her, the more I want to. "Goddesses aren't defined by their beauty. They're defined by their power. You have that, yet you react to the world instead of commanding it."

I don't know why I'm telling her this, but it's been weighing on me since the first night I saw her play.

Maybe I see something in her I recognize, the feeling she's been wronged and is trying—futilely, desperately—to set things right.

"Easy for you to say," she replies. "People wait for you to act. By the time I have a chance, they've already made up their mind about me. Already decided things that change my present and my future."

The earnest way she's watching me, like my words are sinking in, has my chest tightening.

"Learn to take your power and no one can tell you what to do."

Her dark lashes blink as she cradles her chin between her palms, inhaling slowly before letting the breath out.

"Well, damn. Thanks for the career advice, Mr. King," she says, deadpan.

Insolent. Instead of offering her the chance to

play Debajo, I could've let her languish in the obscurity she brought on herself.

And she's repaying me with insults.

When her lips twitch in a smirk, a jolt of lust snaps down my spine.

I said I wanted to bring her peace.

I take it back.

I want to shut up that mouth that delights in insulting me, my cock, and the empire I've built. To watch those dark eyes cloud when I shove her back on this table, drag the denim off her legs and make her explode on my tongue.

It's the first I've wanted a woman this powerfully in months, the first I've pictured what it would feel like to take my pleasure alongside hers.

But it's attraction.

Meaningless. Harmless.

It won't control me.

I reach across her for the mug. The next sip I take is better than the first. "No. Thank you."

"For what?" Rae shifts back in her seat, wary.

It's my turn to grin. "For the coffee."

I head for the stairs, sandwich in one hand and mug in the other.

She's still growling when I reach the top step.

8

———

HARRISON

Security at Debajo is surprised to see me twice in four days.

I make my way to the private balcony, waving off the offer of a drink. After the week I've had, though, I sorely want one. Between meetings and business dinners, plus an overnight to London, I've barely been home enough to confirm the villa still stands. But today I did my business, worked out, put on my suit, and here I am.

In fact, I have a plan to advance my business agenda that will happen this weekend.

I told Rae to take her power.

It's about damned time I did the same.

The man who's been avoiding taking my calls about his club can't avoid me any longer...

He's hosting a charity gala at his home, and I'm invited.

On my way in, I checked the door with Leni—lower than Thursday.

I shouldn't be disappointed. There was no earthly reason to believe a twenty-something woman could do what my PR team couldn't.

I'm listening to the opening DJ and entertaining a group of visiting businessmen from Australia in my booth when my phone buzzes in my pocket.

The letters blur at the sides as my eyes adjust in the dark.

Ash: Where are you?

Harry: Debajo.

Ash: I'm worried about you. We both know what day it is.

Harry: I'm fine.

. . .

Ash: High functioning human being fine or drowning your sorrows in expensive liquor fine?

I frown. Of course he's thinking about it too. Not even the French-press coffee—which I've been having the past three days—could snap me out of my melancholy this morning.

I don't respond, and another text comes moments later.

Ash: Speaking of problems, Christian's gala this weekend. Will Mischa be there?

Harrison: He had better not be.

I need to get important business done with our host.

Mischa Ivanov's presence would be more than a complication.

I'd rather eat glass than be in that room with my business rival—both because the business I want to do is more easily conducted without him and because of the woman who's been publicly on his arm for months.

I shove the phone back in my pocket, feeling the change in energy in the club before I look up.

Rae is in the booth, and suddenly I get the "American Dream" theme Leni has been pushing all weekend on social.

Tonight my little American is wearing a platinum wig and a white halter-neck vest and trousers, like a girl-next-door Marilyn Monroe pinup. Except her hair is twisted and spiked.

Not a goddess. A monster.

An arrogant Medusa.

In a room full of people trying to attract one another, she's practically daring anyone look too long.

I shift over the railing, entranced.

When I brought her here, I did my due diligence. I wouldn't let just anyone play my club. But now, watching her play…

Her music lacks the echoing numbness of house tracks. It's melodic. Intimate.

I've only seen her a few times since the run in that left me drinking her coffee and imagining how she tasted instead.

But all of my suits in my wardrobe are accounted for and the pool hasn't acquired any new textiles to clog the filter, so I suppose that's progress.

I stay for the set, half listening to the men I'm

entertaining while inwardly hoping Rae can weave the same spell on me that she weaves on the crowd.

I want to forget the things Mischa Ivanov has done. The things I said to my mother before she died. The vows I made after, that they wouldn't die in vain.

To give up every shred of my own expectations and lose myself in what this woman is creating.

After a few tracks, I look over to see her pressing a hand to her head like she did in the kitchen.

She said it wasn't withdrawal.

Whatever it is, I'm not taking chances.

I motion to security upstairs, pointing at the stage. "Get her water."

"Mr. King, I'm sure there's water—"

"I want a fucking line of them. Enough to hydrate a platoon."

He nods and speaks into his walkie. Moments later, one of the bartenders arrives at the stage with a champagne bucket full of waters on ice.

At the end of the next track, she glances at the waters, then back to her computer.

She transitions into a mashup, "Diamonds are a Girl's Best Friend" mixed with something R&B.

Then she looks up toward the catwalk and flips both middle fingers in the air.

The crowd erupts. They have no idea who she's calling out, but they get off on her defiance.

Perhaps I'd get off on it too, if I wasn't the one she was defying.

Despite the fact that she refused to eat with me the one time I took dinner at home, and barely acknowledges me when we pass in the house, I notice things.

She's terrible at taking care of herself. Lives on fumes. Doesn't go to bed until four or five—I was up one night and saw her light on—even when she doesn't have a show.

That might be fine for a group of college students on holiday, but for a professional who does this year-round? It's unsustainable.

By the end of her set, I haven't seen her touch the water. It's concerning.

"Bring her to the VIP," I tell security.

I'm waiting there, halfway through a poker game, when I feel the presence at my back.

But when I turn, it's security, alone.

"Señor King, she did not want to come."

I drop my cards and leave my chips where they are as I shift out of my chair with a nod to the other players—rich businessmen and VIPs all of them. I grab my jacket off my chair and shrug into it.

"Where is she?"

He doesn't immediately answer, and I take off through the halls.

She's still taking selfies with patrons.

Concern replaces my irritation when I see the fatigue on her face. Security shadows me, but I wave them off as I cut through the crowd to her.

"I told security to bring you back."

She glances at me but poses with her fan. "I didn't want to."

Frustration clashes with the other emotions inside me today—loss, grief, sadness.

"You looked unwell."

Her grin is as aggressive as her spiked hair. "Unwell? I tore the roof off your chic basement tonight, and you think I'm unwell?"

She shoves me out of the way and beckons for the next fan.

"Strange. A woman reamed me out recently—and publicly—for avoiding taking care of someone who was my business," I bite out as the fan takes a selfie, Rae muttering an apology when her hair nearly pokes the man in the face before he heads on his way.

I dismiss the small line of eager fans waiting, ignoring their protests as I grab my DJ's wrist and tug her after me toward the back door.

On the way, I snatch a water bottle off the bar and shove it at her chest.

When we're outside, fresh air washing over us both, she rounds on me. "I can't handle this tonight."

"Because I give a shit whether you pass out on stage or in the middle of a crowd?"

"You don't care about me. I saw you up there, hosting a dozen men exactly like you. All you care about is whether I'm making you money."

My summer home has turned into a hostile place. I'm walking on eggshells in a house with my damned name on the deed.

If I'm going to keep her around, it would be easier if she didn't think I was the devil.

"Follow me." I walk to my Ferrari Roma, then ball up my jacket and throw it in the rear seat as I shift into the front.

The seat molds to my body as I lean back against the headrest and wait.

Seconds tick by.

Finally, the passenger door clicks open, and she shifts inside. "Are you taking me somewhere to kill me?"

"Would've been far easier to do it in your sleep."

"You don't do things the easy way either."

I start the car and shift into gear and pull out of the parking lot.

"My parents died of an overdose. Both of them,

the same night. Fourteen years ago. That's why I don't tolerate drugs in my business."

I grip the wheel tighter as I navigate the streets.

"I'm sorry."

Her voice is low, the contrition genuine.

"You didn't know?"

It was in endless media outlets at the time. They were senior executives at a massive international organization, plus visible contributors to a dozen charitable organizations in the UK and abroad.

"I would've been ten."

Fair enough.

She leans an arm against the window. "The pills you found were prescription. For anxiety. I haven't taken them regularly for months, but I like having them just in case."

Relief blurs with guilt.

"Why were they in an unmarked bottle? And in your checked bag, for God's sake?"

"Why not? I wasn't expecting the airline to lose my suitcase."

I navigate to a place I would know with my eyes closed, then I pull into the parking lot.

I shift out of the car and retrieve a bottle of Glen Scotia from the boot. "The first time we came to Ibiza, I was eleven. Ash was a baby. My parents bought a villa here when I was thirteen. I lost my virginity in that house."

Rae shuts the passenger door. "I hope she was well paid."

The laughter rips from deep inside my chest. I don't let anyone make fun of me.

Just this once, I allow it.

My companion shifts up onto the hood and turns to look out over the sand and surf. "They left it to you when they passed?"

I shake my head. "They would have. But their assets were tied up."

I take a long swig of whisky, the warmth scorching my throat like a welcome friend. Rae waves me off when I hold the bottle out to her.

"My parents didn't own nightclubs, but they managed real estate for a large Russian investor. When I was a teenager, they found out their employer was into... less than legal side busi-nesses. They told him they wanted to go out on their own. Even purchased a venue under their own name."

My chest tightens. They were optimistic about the possibility of working for themselves.

"Their employer wouldn't let them. The project burned down, and the investigation ruled they had burned it down to collect the insurance. As a result, they collected no compensation. A few months later, my parents were dead of an over-dose, but they didn't use drugs."

I feel her attention on me, the shocked stare. I don't know why I'm telling her except that I haven't fucking told anyone in a long time, and today of all days, I can think of little else.

"I vowed I would clear their name and rebuild what they'd lost—in my own way. So, when you say I only care about making money... you're wrong. I care about restoring their legacy. Putting right what should have been. I won't apologize for that."

The tightness in my throat, in my chest, won't release.

"This was my mother's favorite beach. We came every year for her birthday." I lean forward, brace my elbows on my knees. "I still do."

Rae shifts toward me, the moonlight catching the highlights in her hair.

"That's what today is," she says softly, and I nod.

Her presence shouldn't feel comforting, but it does.

Strange how the same woman can bring me madness and peace.

"So why bring me?"

I lace my fingers together as I listen to the waves crash against the shore, watch the lights of the city reflected in the distance. "This is a place to escape your demons. Or entertain them. You seem like a person who does both."

Rae shifts off the car, taking the bottle from my hand. She tugs off her shoes and tosses them back at me. I grab them out of the air so they don't land on the hood of my car.

I follow her out onto the sand. "Give me the whisky."

"Come get it."

There's only one other couple within sight on the beach, locked in a heated embrace. Her gaze lingers on them, and I take advantage, catching up and taking the bottle, then rewarding myself with a long drink.

"This is known as a romantic place," I inform her.

Rae rolls up her trousers and steps up to the edge of the ocean, her teeth flashing white in the dark. "So, you didn't bring me here to kill me. You brought me here to fuck me."

I chuckle. "You're a porcupine, and it's not only your hair. I wouldn't stick my cock anywhere near you for fear it would come back covered in quills."

Her low laugh ripples across the sound of the waves.

I'm starting to think it would be worth it.

I wonder who I'd find when I stripped away

her clothes. The woman she is on stage, or the one in a T-shirt and jeans with a bottle of anxiety pills to keep her company?

Perhaps both.

I want to find out.

So fucking much.

I reach for the buttons on my shirt, undoing one after another. Then I toss the shirt at her head.

She catches the fabric, looking up in surprise.

I'm already working on my trousers, unfastening and unzipping them before shoving them down.

Her gaze lingers on my body. "Is this how you get women?"

"Let's find out."

I'm nostalgic and buzzed, and the way she's looking at me helps both.

The cool water licks my feet and ankles as I stop in front of her. "Admit you want me," I challenge. "I won't tell a soul."

She pries the alcohol from my grip. "I told you —the only way you'll ever get me naked is to sue the clothes off me."

My hands close over hers on the bottle. She doesn't let go.

I back into the surf, and her grip means she's forced to follow. "That could still be arranged."

Rae's lips curve in the dark as the water rises up her body.

It soaks her trousers. Her stomach. I don't stop until water reaches my abs and her chest, and I feel the tug of the undercurrent.

The exhilaration on her face is interrupted by shock when she notices the marks on my chest.

"What is this?" She nods to my pec, the mass of white lines there.

"Prison tattoo."

She looks up in alarm, realizing I'm joking when she sees my expression.

"It's a scar from boarding school," I amend.

Her brows tug together. "You let another person do this to you?"

"'Let' is a strong word. Boys can be cruel."

"Anyone can be cruel."

The water is up to her ribs, high enough it licks at her breasts when a wave rolls through, leaves her top stained and her nipples hard against the fabric when it recedes.

I want to trace the path with a finger.

Maybe my tongue.

"I didn't mean it."

Her words have me jerking my gaze up to meet hers.

"About your ex-fiancée and that you deserved for her to leave you."

I pull the bottle toward me and take a drink. "I thought I was in love. She was a spoiled princess. We wanted different things."

She takes the bottle back but not to drink it. It bobs in the water at her side, her grip on its neck assuring it doesn't drift away.

I reach a hand out experimentally to touch one of the spikes in her hair.

It's sharp.

"Your brother said you dated her because you thought she was what you deserved."

Her voice is low, but the words land in my chest as my hand falls away.

She's young.

Too fucking young to ask questions like that.

My attention drifts down her body exposed by the water. Her lips, full and parted. Her shoulders, dripping with the sea.

It's all there on her face. The vulnerability she hides under sarcasm and barbs.

"On stage when you play, you're generous," I murmur. "Are you so generous when you fuck?"

Rae's eyes widen as she holds my gaze for a heartbeat. Two.

What I'm feeling is attraction, but it's more than that. It's reckless. A need no amount of money can solve, a question no woman but this one can answer.

She backs slowly out of the water, and my gaze sticks to her body even as she reaches the shore.

"What are you doing?" I rasp.

Rae bends toward the sand, every curve hugged by her wet clothes. When she straightens, something glinting in her hand, her slow smile catches me off guard.

"I need your keys, King. Because you're drunk and I'm driving."

9

RAE

The car is built for speed, but I'm more aware of the man in the passenger seat than the roar of the engine. He's still distractingly naked from the waist up, his arm resting on the windowsill.

"Turn right," he says.

"I know."

"You're an insolent chauffeur."

"I'd be more pleasant if you rode in the back." I spare a glance for the impossibly cramped rear seat of the Ferrari.

My companion's grin is quick and surprised, but my gaze falls to the scars on his chest once more. Evidence of something I never entertained...

Harrison King is human.

I don't know what to do with that information, except wish I could forget it.

But I can't.

His parents died, suddenly and horrifically, and took everything he knew of life with them. He started over from nothing with only a vision of what might have been to keep him company.

I know how lonely it is to rebuild your world once it's shattered. I've felt the grief that comes with losing not only your security, but yourself.

We make it back to the house and park in front of the villa.

He reaches over me and hits a button on the car's dash, opening the trunk. I shift out of the car as he retrieves his bottle of liquor from the trunk, then I follow him up the steps to the front door.

At night, the villa is breathtaking. This entire place feels like a magical escape.

Harrison turns to me on the landing and holds out a hand. I place the keys in his open palm, and he closes his fingers so fast I jump.

"What are you thinking?" he murmurs.

"I'm wondering if you always keep a bottle of liquor in your car."

His eyes crinkle at the corners. "Only today."

We head inside, finding Barney waiting in the low nightlights of the kitchen. Harrison leans down to pat the eager pet before grabbing a lowball glass from the kitchen shelf and starting toward the stairs, glass in one hand and bottle in the other.

I don't think it's a good idea for him to drink more, or alone, given what this day means to him. "I want a sandwich," I blurt.

It'll keep him from drinking, plus put real food in his stomach in case he continues.

"You're asking the wrong man." But he pauses on the first step long enough that I try something crazy.

"Please?"

With a wary look, as if he's guessing what I'm playing at, Harrison relents and crosses to the fridge.

The dog makes a hopeful noise as the door opens.

"Natalia keeps the good stuff in here," he murmurs, pulling on a drawer.

"She hides it from you?"

"Used to when we were kids. I ate anything in sight for a few years."

He uses the fresh bread on the counter and serrano and hard cheese from the fridge to make two sandwiches.

Claiming seats on opposite sides of the table, we eat in silence.

This is the longest we've gone without sparring.

"Enjoying the view?" He catches me checking him out, and I swallow my bite and nearly my tongue along with it.

"Your brother's hotter," I manage.

Harrison lifts a brow.

"What? He's my age." I shift in my seat. "Unlike you."

Blue eyes cool on mine. "Don't let me stand in your way."

The comment shouldn't disappoint me. It does.

Tonight, he looked at me like I was more than means to an end.

It was unexpected and thrilling.

We finish our snacks, and Harrison offers the last piece of meat to Barney, who spins in a delighted circle.

"You don't strike me as the dog type."

"My brother bought him for me after Eva left." Harrison takes our plates and sets them on the counter.

"Said he was to keep me company," he goes on, "but I think he wanted to soften me."

We start for the stairs, Harrison gesturing for me to go first.

He's behind me, so close that if I turned, we'd

be touching. His strong chest and arms, those unearthly blue eyes, his vile, gorgeous mouth.

"Did it work?" I ask over a shoulder.

The house is quiet except for Barney's soft whining from the floor below. As if he feels the tension from his spot on the rug by the door.

"You tell me."

When we get to the top, I pause and turn.

He's right there. Beautiful and messed up and filling my senses.

When I lift my chin to meet Harrison's gaze, we're breathing the same air. His mouth is inches away, his bare chest too. All that power carefully restrained.

"As a boy, I wondered if the people who are softest on the inside are hardest on the outside."

"Why is that?" I manage.

His eyes are deep as the ocean, guarded emotions swirling beneath the surface like rogue currents.

"Because they have to be."

I never claimed to be in exceptional shape, but as I pull up at the end of my run on Friday, I'm breathing heavily while Barney barely pants.

"I'm sending you some money," I tell Callie as I ruffle the fur on the dog's head.

I've played three shows in Ibiza and been paid for the first two. True to his word, Harrison cut me in—though the door was nowhere near enough to make a dent in the twenty thousand, which means I need to haul ass to fill the place the rest of the time I'm here.

"I would never have asked you if it wasn't—"

"I know," I say. "It's important to both of us. How is work?"

Her voice is instantly more enthusiastic as she talks about the young women she's met during the past week at an event she ran.

The past few days, I've been feeling better too. Working on social media, on my sets, and even meeting up with Leni to get ideas for how to draw more people to Debajo.

I'm more comfortable now that I have my belongings back.

Minus the pills. I still find myself looking over to the nightstand for them at least once a day.

"So, how are the guys?" Callie's voice drags me back. "Any hot locals or all tourists?"

I can't tell if it's the steep hill leading up to the villa or the memory of swimming with Harrison King that has my heart hammering.

The man who kept my mind whirring long after I crawled into bed Monday night, body still tingling from the sea and his presence and driving his car, isn't a tourist or a local. He's a globe-trotting billionaire who hides himself behind his thirst for conquering.

Are you generous when you fuck?

Under the half moon, far from the lights of Ibiza Town, the question floored me.

Not because of his hard body or physical intensity, but because he showed me a piece of his soul, then leaned in.

What he told me about his parents' deaths, how everything he does is devoted to building what they could've had…

I can't help looking at him through a new lens.

Which hardly matters because since that night, he's been avoiding me.

I'm sure if I pinned him down, he'd say he's been occupied with work and dinners out.

But Thursday morning, I was up earlier than usual and tripped into the hallway in my pajamas to use the bathroom only to run into him emerging in his towel, clean and unshaven.

He caught the fabric before it slipped too far, but I could see the trail of light hair from his navel downward.

If I thought the night in the ocean was dangerous, this was indecent.

He looked startled to see me awake, muttering about his showerhead being replaced in the ensuite while I tried not to choke on my own tongue.

When he didn't attend my show that night, I was disappointed.

The door inched up as a result of video streamed from the previous performance. I should've been relieved there was no moody owner to keep me from talking with fans and helping ensure next week's gig would be even bigger.

I wasn't.

Since the richest man I've ever met made me sandwiches half-naked in his kitchen, he's been dodging me like a high school quarterback who's dealing with one too many irritating crushes.

"Rae, you're not responding. That means there's a guy."

"He's not my type," I say as I reach the door of the villa and push it open, going for the dog's leash before my shoes. Lesson learned on that front.

"I'm everyone's type," a familiar voice calls from the living room.

"I know you took a hit to your career by standing up to King," she goes on, "but it speaks to the kind of person you are. You deserve a hot summer fling."

Guilt gnaws at my stomach.

Maybe I could stand to get laid. But I roll with guys more likely to sell their belongings for a ticket to an indie music festival than count the money from their international conquests.

Even if my body thinks the man would make a beautiful distraction, it's wrong. I'm here to do this job.

Not to fuck him.

After saying goodbye to my cousin, I hang up and cross to where Ash is stretched out along the couch watching sports.

"What is this place, the headquarters of the British Billionaires Club?" I mutter.

"Charming. But I'm a future member, not a current one."

His smile is contagious as he gestures to the couch next to him. I drop into the spot, still sweaty from my run.

"I told you you'd stay," he gloats. "I trust my brother charmed you into it?"

"Not quite. We came to a new agreement that worked for everyone. Why are you here? Don't you have a hotel?"

"I'm staying at a villa with guys from my club. Though once you spend an entire season with a bunch of pricks, you've had enough of them by the end."

"Then why did you come to Ibiza with them?"

Ash frowns. "One of the veterans is trying to turn the club against me. I had a reputation for being perfectionistic when I was drafted. It served me fine my entire life, but apparently teammates don't like my standards applied to them. It's like fucking secondary school all over again."

"This is why I never made friends in high school." When Ash starts to rise from the couch, I tug him back down. "People decide what they want from you. You have to show them they're wrong."

He holds out his coffee. "Try this. Natalia got it."

"Natalia didn't get it. I did."

Ash cocks his head. "Brilliant American girl."

Harrison walks in, looking between us. The tension on his face deepens. "You two are lying around all day?"

Ash puts his hands behind his head. "Just waiting for you to come and judge us."

His brother shoots him a look that could freeze an active volcano before glancing my way.

No sign of a thaw.

He's gone the next instant.

"It's not you," Ash says. "There's a charity gala event tomorrow night and major players Harrison needs to show face with."

Curiosity has me leaning in. "And he doesn't

want to?"

"Only because his business rival might be there."

"The man your parents used to work for."

Ash shifts back to one end of the couch, surveying me with surprise.

"He told me he wants to build an empire to atone for what happened to your parents. What he thinks happened to them."

Ash nods, still looking impressed by my knowledge. "Our parents worked for the Ivanov family. Now their son has taken over the business."

"Harrison thinks they had a hand in your parents' deaths."

Ash flinches. "Wealth and power make people do strange things."

I shake my head, trying to catch up. "Mischa and Harrison are the same age?"

"Two years apart. But they went to school together." Ash frowns. "This gala is a bore, but the host is a friend of the family." His expression brightens. "Come with me as my date."

I snort, until I realize he's serious.

"Can I wear this?" I gesture to my running clothes, and he barks out a laugh.

"Fuck no. It's black tie. I'll pick you up at eight!" he calls as I head to my room, taking down my hair and eager to shower off the sweat.

Before I can, my gaze flicks to the nightstand, and I do a double take at the bottle of pills there.

Same medication. Same dosage. Enough to last me until I leave.

What the...?

He's been avoiding me all week. No more.

I head down the hall and push in Harrison's office door without knocking.

He looks up from his desk, looking caught out but otherwise immaculate in a pale-green shirt that sets off his blond hair and slight tan.

"You replaced my pills," I say.

"I estimated the dosage based on the size of the ones I disposed of."

I turn toward his bookshelves. The fact that this man knows more than anyone about my weaknesses has my stomach clenching.

"Thank you. I like knowing they're there if I need them."

It's almost as if they're an artifact from a version of me that no longer exists but one I don't want to forget.

There are dozens of books, and I trace a finger along the faded spines before I pull out one in a clear plastic case. "*The Count of Monte Cristo.* A good man who lost his way on a path for vengeance."

"Vindication. Justice. There's a difference."

I open the cover and take in the date, my mouth rounding. "A first edition?"

"The first edition was published as a serial and in French. This is a second."

I nearly drop it in my haste to replace it on the shelf.

"Why did you let me pick it up? It's three hundred years old and could fall apart in a second."

"Beautiful things are made to be touched."

The softness in his voice sends shivers through me.

Like that, I'm rocketed back to the night on the beach. His words, his closeness, his intensity.

"I understand from Leni the door was up by a hundred last night," he goes on. "You'll need to do better if you want to profit from our deal."

I frown. "I see our truce is over."

"Were you hoping it wasn't?" He cocks his head.

I refuse to cop to anything where he's concerned. He'll make me pay for it.

"There's something about you I can't figure out."

"Only one thing?"

He ignores me and continues. "What changed from your first night in Ibiza to the next morning that made you renegotiate?"

I don't want to talk about this. It's personal.

But the man who told me about his parents dying two nights ago replaced my anxiety meds.

There isn't a clean line between business and personal with him, if there ever was one.

"My cousin co-runs a program for women who've experienced sexual violence. Their funding has been slashed by government cuts. They need help keeping the lights on for a couple of months, or they won't be able to keep providing services."

He blinks at me as if I told him I wanted to buy breeding rhinoceros and start a farm back in Orange County.

"That's very committed," he says at last. "But you can't take responsibility for everyone in this world. There are too many evils."

Conviction has me standing straighter. "No woman should have to endure sexual violence, and they sure as fuck shouldn't endure it alone."

He studies me long enough that I feel as if he's peering beneath my skin, under the layers of Little Queen or Rae which are fit for public consumption.

He shifts in his chair, his strong body reclining as both hands curl over the armrests. "There's a charity event tomorrow for the local environmental commission. Plenty of cynics like me and bleeding hearts like you."

"I heard. Ash asked me to go with him."

"Ash?" Surprise flits across his handsome face. Harrison rubs a hand over his jaw. "Tell my brother he can find another date. You'll go with me."

I laugh, incredulous. "What? Why?"

"I can want the company of an earnest young music producer in my employ. Who knows? Perhaps you can elicit business for your show next week."

I could promote Debajo, but that would mean being the date of this man I respond to when I shouldn't. Fancy clothes, booze, Harrison King looking like the god he is while he wraps Ibiza's in crowd around his finger.

Since my conversation with Callie, I can't help wondering what else he could do with those hands.

Harrison King might boast about his empire, but he has the goods to back it up.

Would he be as capable if he applied himself to a woman?

I know he would.

What I'm less sure of is whether he'd plow through her, demand she bend to his every need until she's so caught up in his storm she can't resist it...

Or whether he'd check his ambition long

enough to learn and explore and test and play.

To step out of his need for power like I watched him step out of his clothes that night at the beach.

I swallow.

Spending a night with him would be more than a quick fix. I can't let him get under my skin more than he already has.

"I don't think so."

His gaze narrows as he folds his arms across his chest. "You don't *want* to spend an evening with me."

I cross to his desk, lift the letter opener off the blotter, and hold it out. "In case you need help scraping yourself off the ground."

But before I can turn, a hand closes around my wrist, hot and firm and strong.

"I said it would be more appropriate if you dated my brother. That wasn't a suggestion."

"Really? You're so damned subtle it's hard to keep up," I taunt.

Bad idea.

His thumb brushes the underside of my wrist. Soft, deliberate.

My pulse leaps in response, and the letter opener clatters to the desktop.

"I need a date, and you owe me three favors," he drawls. I don't realize I've stopped breathing until he releases me again. "Consider this the first."

10

RAE

This is a bad fucking idea.

I take a deep breath as I turn back to the mirror. The dress is the color of tangerines, ripe and lush.

It's cut high at the front, circling my neck like a collar. The back is nonexistent, starting above the top of my ass. The skirt has a high slit up one thigh, and the long fabric on either side ripples when I turn or walk.

Before I could ask Ash what to wear or browse shops on my own, the box appeared on my bed.

The sky-high wedge sandals that came with the dress are the same color as my skin. They're uncomfortable as hell when I fasten them around my ankles, but before I can decide whether to take them off, a knock sounds on my door.

"I understand most women consider tardiness a virtue, but I didn't expect it of you," comes the grumpy British voice from the other side.

I pull it open an inch, and my chest contracts.

Harrison King is breathtaking in his tux. James Bond come to life, with a hard body, sculpted lips, strong hands, and eyes that promise to steal your secrets and keep them for himself.

But it's the naked hunger on his face when he sees me, his gaze dragging over me like he's starved, that makes me want to turn around and slam the door.

"It's more Little Queen than me," I quip to hide the ripples of awareness.

"She's you. And this..." His gaze runs down my figure again. "This is definitely you."

His praise warms me. I don't need anyone else's approval, but knowing a man who's seen every-thing, done everything, could have anyone, gets simple pleasure from being in my presence is a high I never expected.

"You arseholes coming, or should Toro and I go on ahead?" Ash taunts from down the stairs.

When I start along the open hallway, Ash spots me from the foyer and dining area below and whistles. "Christ, Rae. If you're looking for a man tonight—"

"She's not," Harrison informs him.

I make it down the hall without incident, then trip at the top of the stairs. Strong arms grab my waist, my ribs, before I can spill down to the first floor.

"Are the shoes the wrong size?" Harrison murmurs at my ear.

"No. They're the wrong style." I go on at his confused look. "If I wanted eight more inches, I'd have asked for it."

"And I'd have given it to you," Ash declares, making me grin and Harrison glare.

Toro greets us outside. "Beautiful," he says, beaming at me.

"Thanks. I had the dress in my suitcase." I wink, and he laughs. "What about this car?" I nod to the vintage Rolls-Royce, a departure from the usual Mercedes, complete with a chrome ornament on the hood.

"Had it in my basement," he teases, and it's my turn to grin.

Since I arrived in Ibiza, we've found a handful of moments to talk. In the car, I learned Natalia is his wife and that they've worked for Harrison's family a long time. One day, when I found him working in the garden outside, I insisted he let me help him. In exchange, he told me about his daughter.

He misses her. It's clear from the way he speaks about her.

But he and Natalia enjoy taking care of the house, and Harrison and Ash are extended family to them.

Toro goes to help me into the back of the car, but Harrison holds the door first. I shift into the middle, Ash claiming the other side.

"This is cozy," Ash says pleasantly.

We're pressed tight, my shoulders brushing both of theirs. But it's Harrison's I'm most aware of, his body that makes mine tingle.

"So, whose place is this?" I ask, trying to settle my nerves.

"Christian Geroux. A businessman," Harrison states.

He looks as if he's going to say more but pulls out his phone and frowns at it.

When Ash leans forward to talk with Toro, I glance at Harrison's screen, doing a double take. "Whoa. That font is size a million."

"What are you talking about? It's barely legible."

"You need reading glasses."

Harrison presses his lips together and refuses to say more as we head to the party, his strong profile a dark outline against the lights beyond the car.

The idea he has a weakness pisses him off like a business deal gone sour. I smirk the whole way to the party.

The villa we pull up in front of is every bit as sprawling and impressive as the one I'm staying in. More formally designed and decorated, it's meant to be enjoyed by guests as opposed to the people who occupy it when the lights go out.

There are terraced gardens flanking a curved driveway, discreet security in tuxedos at either side of the door. Twinkling lights are just visible on some patio along the side.

We head in through the front door, staff immediately descending to offer us drinks. I'm distracted from the sudden surge of nerves by the gorgeous house, every wall filled with art, every corner with lush plants.

On the terrace, a hundred people are milling about. There's a six-piece band in one corner and a dance floor. Torches light the huge outside space, with recessed lighting on the inside.

"This place is incredible," I murmur to Ash.

"Christian had it built as his holiday home. He spared no expense. He never does."

Before long, people are approaching us—approaching Harrison mostly. When pressed, he introduces me as Raegan. No one calls me Raegan, but as unsettling as it is, there's something new about it on his lips.

I'd been expecting Harrison to be distant like in the car or confrontational like every other time, but he's the opposite. He stands close enough to steer me with a hand on my back, but his presence feels protective rather than controlling.

For a minute, I wonder what it would feel like to be on his arm for real. He's a king here, and not only in name. This world he plays in, he runs it.

The men he considers rivals must be formidable indeed.

One of the women smiles in my direction as Harrison and her husband, who's in media, talk global news and business. It's a strange vibe as she leans in. "Do you model?"

I choke on my drink. "Not lately."

"Ah. Harrison is a master at keeping beautiful women on his arm. But I suppose things change."

Her catty tone makes me stiffen. Next to me, Harrison glances over in the middle of his sentence. As if he didn't hear but sensed my reaction.

A hand on my back has awareness tingling up my spine.

"You know," I say to her, "I was reading a story last week about how this wine tasting club was served the wrong wine. Instead of a thousand-dollar bottle, they got a twenty-dollar one. And they gave it rave reviews."

"I don't follow."

"Quality doesn't come from a label," Harrison cuts in smoothly.

The fact that he was listening enough to stay on top of my conversation, not only his, has gratitude blooming in my stomach.

He leans in, brushing his lips against my ear. "Everything all right?"

"I can handle them."

"I know you can. But that doesn't mean you should have to." He squeezes my arm, a brief reassurance as genuine as it is surprising.

I'm not comfortable at large events. Unless I'm performing, where I have distance from the crowd, I prefer small groups with people I know.

When I stopped going to parties in high school, around the same time I started working on my music, I figured my friends would understand.

They didn't.

The girls who used to invite me to things turned their backs on me.

When I tried to explain that I couldn't relax and enjoy myself, they froze me out.

Evidently our friendship was based on gushing over our older brothers' college friends, and getting drunk enough we couldn't remember what we did the next day.

Once neither of those things appealed to me, I stopped appealing to them.

Tonight, Harrison's telling me he knows I've got this. But in case I don't, he's got me.

It's that realization that has me pulling back. "I, ah, need to find a bathroom."

I duck out, feeling his gaze between my shoulders.

On the way, I get lost and run into a distinguished-looking man in his seventies.

"Good evening. We haven't met," he says, reaching for my hand.

I let him take it, press a dry kiss to the back. "I was just looking for a bathroom," I say when he releases me.

"*Bien sûr.* This is my house, and I can show you the way."

"Oh! Mr. Geroux."

"Christian, please." He graciously spreads his hands. "Make yourself at home. I do enjoy hosting, and I'll have fewer opportunities when I retire."

"Then why retire at all?"

"Because I have children who require me unlike any business. For some of us, it's a pleasure to build and acquire and possess. A game. For

others, it's their life—they need to prove themselves, to redeem themselves."

Christian's eyes gleam. "My ventures are like
my children. I will miss certain ones more than
others. La Mer is a once-in-a-lifetime place."

My heart kicks. "You own La Mer?"

"For thirty years. You've heard of it." He looks
genuinely pleased.

"It's exquisite. I've always wanted to—" I cut
myself off before saying "play there." "Attend."

"You must while you are here. As my guest,
before I sell to one of its many suitors." He hands
me a card. "Give this to the men at the door, and
we will let you in." He pats my arm as we arrive at
the bathroom door.

But as I thank him and head inside, my head is
spinning.

Harrison's here to see the man who owns La
Mer, which can only mean one thing—he's here
trying to buy it.

This is what he's been working on all week
while he's been avoiding me. Judging by how big
this deal must be, I bet he's been working on it far
longer than that.

And what of his rival? Does the Ivanov family
want La Mer just as much?

I know what it's like to have your past snapping
at your heels, but it's bigger for Harrison.

If tonight is as important as it sounds, why did he go to such lengths to bring me as his date?

The only thing I can think is that I'd be a distraction for the other partygoers. A tacky novelty.

Except I remember the way his hand felt on my back. How genuine he sounded when he wanted to make sure I was okay.

Everything I learn about him makes me more confused, and more drawn to him.

I touch up my lipstick in the mirror, still surprised by the woman looking back at me.

She might not be a goddess, but she's different than she was two weeks ago.

I have a career again. A club that's starting to feel like mine, that's doing better thanks to me.

I have people to smile and laugh with.

And tonight...

I have a date with a man who's complicated and sexy and a worthy opponent.

Why not enjoy it a little?

My shoes are rubbing in all the wrong places as I head down the hallway, intent on finding Harrison.

His voice reaches my ears at the same time as the music far away. I can't make out the words, but I spot him in a corner, speaking to a stunning blonde. She's statuesque, like an old movie star with perfect hair and perfect curves.

It's her voice I make out first. "It's not the same without you."

When she reaches for him, laying a hand on his face—that coolly untouchable face—every thought evaporates.

I watch them for a minute, my chest aching in protest as he murmurs a response too low to hear.

For a moment, on his arm, I felt as if this world was mine too. To borrow, if not to own.

But seeing Harrison in a moment of obvious intimacy with the woman I assume is his ex reminds me I'm an outsider.

I don't know this man. I can't, and I shouldn't want to. Just because he's capable of being close with someone doesn't mean I should expect him to do anything other than hurt me or disappoint me.

I take off the uncomfortable shoes and leave them in a corner behind a potted plant. As I start down the hall, I run into Ash.

"You should've come with me, American Girl," he tosses.

"I shouldn't have come at all."

His grin fades as I grab a drink off a passing tray.

"Tell him I'm heading out," I say. "If he notices I'm gone."

Harrison

I told myself I wouldn't feel a thing the next time I saw her.

I was wrong.

"Do you remember how we used to lie out all day sunbathing in Monaco?" Eva asks.

It's not as if I still care for her, but the echoes of it fill my chest when I thought I'd burnt them out and remind me of something important.

I'm capable of caring.

"Where is your date this evening?" I interrupt.

"Singapore. Or maybe Tokyo." She waves a dismissive hand as if his absence makes him unworthy of discussion.

I glance past her. "If this is your attempt to keep me from speaking with Christian—"

"Of course not! I hoped I'd see you tonight."

Her soft pout used to get to me, but now, in the hall where she's cornered me, I see only the manipulation beneath.

"Well, now you have. Give my regards to your new diversion for me."

I brush past her down the hall, determined to find Christian.

Though my primary purpose tonight is to pin down our host, I can't stop thinking about the woman who excused herself from my side twenty minutes ago and hasn't returned since.

As I pass impeccably dressed guests in tuxes and dresses in every color of the rainbow, my mind flashes back to my reluctant date handling herself in the den of rich vipers.

I'd half expected the seething sullenness she'd graced me with more than once, but in this exclusive crowd, she was both gracious and assertive.

It pleased me.

Everything about her tonight pleased me from the second she stepped out of her room in that dress looking even more stunning than I'd expected.

After spending my mother's birthday with Rae, I did avoid her for the better part of the week.

Not because she'd done something wrong—on the contrary, I was thinking about her too damned much.

But when I learned my brother planned to bring her tonight as his date, something inside me broke.

The same part of me that purred with satisfaction when I drew her against my side, caressed her back with my hand like it was my right.

None of it means anything. Not compared to the reason I'm here.

I force her from my mind as I reach the doors of the library, spotting my quarry inside surrounded by a circle of men.

"How good to see you, Harrison." Christian's gaze lands on me, and everyone parts to let me in.

I extend a hand, which he takes. That's their cue to leave, and they depart.

"Let me guess," Christian says, accepting a fresh drink from a waiter once the other guests have pulled the library doors closed behind them. "You're here to talk about football?"

"I'll leave that to my brother. No, I'm here to remind you that you're going to sell me La Mer."

He sighs. "Harrison... I've known you for two decades. Ambition has always been a strength. But as an old man, I'm telling you to find other things in your life. My children are my joy now. Did you meet my Sylvie?"

I mentally scan the faces from the party, vaguely recalling a pretty young woman who greeted us near the door. "Yes. Lovely."

"She is. My other children are settled, but I worry for her."

"The young have a way of surprising you. She'll find her way."

I glance out the window and spot the glowing orange dress, Rae's dark hair in waves around her shoulders.

It's refreshing to see her without a costume beyond the dress I chose for her.

But as she trips down the steps, alarm has my abs clenching.

Christian follows my gaze, making a sound of muffled surprise. "Perhaps we should finish this conversation another time."

No. We should finish it now.

But as Rae reaches the curved driveway, my feet won't cooperate.

"One moment."

I head out to the hall, pushing through the crowds and ignoring anyone who tries to stop me.

Ash steps in front of me before I reach the front doors. "Don't."

"Don't what? Tell my date she should stay until the end of the party?"

"She said she wished she hadn't come."

A sharpened spear sneaks under my ribs.

I shouldn't fucking care what she thinks, but I'm angry. She said she'd come with me, and she's turning her back on me at the first opportunity.

I shove past Ash and take the steps two at a time.

"Raegan."

She turns, and I soak her in. This time it's not the way she looks in that dress, though she's stunning. It's the expression on her face—hurt and disappointment.

Words always come easily, but now I'm reaching for them. "What happened to your shoes?"

She blinks up at me, ignoring the question. "The woman inside. Your ex, right?" Surprise slams into me, but she continues. "You could've brought her. It looked as if she would've been more than happy to come with you. Or leave with you."

My mind races to process her frosty tone, settling on something as fascinating as it is improbable.

Is she jealous?

Raegan Madani? The woman who ruined her career to score a few points on me?

The possibility fucks me up in the best way.

"I get that the only reason you hired me was to play your club and make back what I cost you," she goes on, and her dark eyes are big enough to swallow me whole. "But you do not get to dress me up and drag me here and *use* me like this."

She points at her bare feet, and the red welts have me wincing.

"You should've told me the shoes didn't fit."

She shoves me, hard enough that I stagger. "I shouldn't have worn them at all! Your stupid favor didn't involve footwear. I came because I said I would, and I thought maybe you wanted me to come with you. Which is crazy. This is your world. These are your rich, entitled people. Enjoy them."

I didn't know I had the ability to hurt this woman. Even Eva, whom I thought I loved, proved to have an icy heart I could never penetrate. But this woman—this girl—who's so extraordinary on a stage and is so stubborn off it...

It makes me wonder what other good things she hides beneath her tough exterior, pretending she cares for nothing and no one.

"I didn't know she'd be here," I say at last. "She left me for Mischa Ivanov. My rival, the man I hate."

Her eyes widen with disbelief. "Your fiancée left you for the man who killed your parents?"

I nod. "She wanted a different kind of power than I offered."

The light from the torches dances along the curved driveway, reflecting in her dark eyes. Emotions collide on her face.

Compassion.

Hurt.

I wish we were alone instead of here at this party.

Fuck it.

I close the distance between us, take her face in my hands.

The surge of adrenaline when I touch her, when we lock gazes, is real.

The pull between us is real.

There's only one woman I wanted on my arm tonight. And since she left it, she's been missed.

A familiar car pulls up the drive, pulling into her peripheral vision, and Rae steps back.

She reaches for the door, but I slam it shut with a hand.

"Don't go," I bite out. "If I've made you feel less in some way, I'm fucking sorry."

I need her to understand how hard I've worked to get what I have, to keep it. That letting a person come between me and my revenge nearly cost me everything.

She pries my fingers off the door one at a time.

"Don't be sorry, Harrison. Be better."

As the car pulls away with her inside, I'm left feeling empty and frustrated in a way that has nothing to do with Christian and the deal.

11

———

RAE

The next morning, there's a message on my social profile asking for an interview.

I message back:

If this is about what happened in the spring, I don't do interviews.

There's a reply almost instantly.

I want to talk about your new gig in Ibiza. You're causing a lot of buzz. When can we meet?

. . .

I've never done face-to-face interviews, which are outside my comfort zone because it's harder to control the conversation, so I tuck the phone away without responding.

I shift out of bed and trip over to the door, catching sight of my still-sprayed hair in the mirror. The makeup that didn't quite come off my face last night after the party.

The party.

It all rushes back. Playing Cinderella. Pretending to be part of that world.

And the feeling of seeing Harrison with his ex.

As I step out into the hall, I expect to hear him, but there's nothing.

His office door is closed, and so is his bedroom.

"Looking for Mr. Moody?" Ash calls from the dining area downstairs.

I lean over the railing. "Maybe. What're you doing here?"

"Got back last night to find our club's villa trashed. Tripped over bottles and naked tourists to come over."

I pad downstairs and eye the green smoothie Ash is drinking. "That looks disgusting."

"So do you." He ruffles my hair. "But last night, you were stunning. Everyone noticed." He pauses. "He left for business this morning."

"Oh." I try not to feel disappointed he didn't tell me. "For how long?"

"Who knows?" His eyes narrow. "But there's something in the kitchen for you."

I look where he's pointing to see a huge stainless-steel espresso maker.

"Shit. Does it do laundry too?" Up close, it's even more impressive, and I run a hand over the levers and dials before reaching for the instruction manual next to it. "He must have decided he likes good coffee," I say as I thumb through the pages.

Ash's snort has me looking up. "Yeah. He bought it for himself," he says dryly.

I set the instructions on top of the machine, spotting a Post-it note stuck to the stainless steel.

There's a number scrawled on it.

Eleven hundred thirteen.

It's the door from Thursday's show—up from eight hundred when we started. Two thousand is capacity, so while it's trending in the right direction, we're nowhere near selling out.

"Maybe he bought it for when he returns?" I wonder aloud.

"If that's what you think, you're daft." Ash is watching me with a grin and folded arms. "There's something going on between you and my brother."

I match his posture. "It's called a grudge."

"That might be how you both started, but it's not why you were upset last night."

"A month off from soccer and you're a shrink?"

He plows on, unmoved. "I was twelve when our parents died. Harry showed up at the door of my boarding school. You know the first thing he said to me?"

I shake my head.

"'No matter what anyone says about them, they loved you. That's all you need to know.'

"That day, everything fell to him, legally and practically. He kept me out of the investigation into their deaths. Dealt with their business interests dissolving. It didn't make him crumble; it made him more resolved. You can call him lots of things, but when he commits to something—someone— he'll see it through or die trying."

My chest aches as I think of Harrison, younger than Ash and I are now, being ripped from his education and confronting not only his parents' deaths but the fallout.

"I still hate him half the time," I admit.

"It's the other half that's interesting." He pauses. "While they were engaged, Eva tried to get Harry to step back from his business, supposedly because she wanted time together. Turns out it was so Mischa could get a toehold in markets where his business was strong.

"La Mer would be the final nail in his coffin. It's the biggest venue in the world, the most prestigious. Harry gets it, Mischa loses. It won't bring our parents back, but he thinks it's something." Ash rubs a hand over his jaw. "Most people want to be near my brother for his money or his reputation. You see the man he could be, like I do."

The invitation hangs between us.

It's impossible to forget that amidst Harrison's compulsive desire to empire-build is a genuine protectiveness for his family, a desire to do right by the people he loves.

Because he does love, in his way.

He put his brother first in a time when he himself was grieving and broken. He buys cars for Toro that the old man adores. Hired Leni as his right-hand woman and allows her to be her quirky self.

Judging by the champagne bucket of waters that arrives when I start to lose myself in a set, he even intervenes on my behalf.

"And if he succeeds in growing his business and buying La Mer, you think he'll be that man?" I ask.

"I think he can let go of his grief and have a chance at it."

I stare at the coffee machine, the encouragement implied by it. "Eleven hundred thirteen isn't enough."

"Enough for what?" Ash demands.

"It's nowhere near," I say, ignoring the question as I grab the note and crumpling it up before tossing it in the trash.

I pull up my social and message the reporter back to say I'll meet her.

Harrison

"This is everything." It's a question, but it comes out like a statement as I stare at the manager of BLUE, my LA club.

"Every incident report filed against the club in the past three years," he says.

The stack must be fifty pages thick.

I flip through and skim dates, names, looking for patterns. The only pattern is that there is none, except perhaps for the bare-bones information.

These aren't "reports." They're bookmarks with handwriting on them.

Judging from the paperwork in front of me, the

staff here sees their primary job as making things go away.

"I asked for this information a month ago," I say.

"I'm sorry, Mr. King. Staffing is tight." He presses his lips together. "There've been budget cuts the last two years—"

"Fine." I'd told my managers to tighten up on existing properties to allow us to expand new operations.

Don't be sorry. Be better.

Rae's words echo in my head.

Traveling on business has never felt strange or lonely, but this week feels like both. I've gotten used to having her around my house and around me.

The gala was days ago, and I can still feel Rae's presence. I swear I catch her scent on the air when I step out of a car or off a plane.

Which is fucking crazy.

Rae's not here, and there's no reason she should be. She's doing what she's supposed to be doing—making me money.

So, why would I give a wardrobe full of designer suits for a glimpse of her across a lobby?

"Mr. King?"

I glance up at the manager's voice, realizing I was staring off into space. "Hire more people.

Whatever you need to ensure this issue is properly addressed."

"Yes, sir. Thank you. Would you like me to send you any new reports?"

I consider it. "Only if you can't manage them yourself. But if I have to make another request for information like this one, they had better be robust fucking accounts. If a patron so much as gets a drink spilled on them—"

"We'll take care of it." He nods as I shift out of the seat and start for the door. "Your car is waiting outside. It's too bad you're leaving LA so soon and can't stay for this evening's show."

I cut a look over my shoulder. "I'll be in Miami tonight."

"Enjoying your venue?"

I smile tightly.

"Doing the same damn thing we did here," I mutter under my breath on my way out.

12

RAE

I'd never believed that a house could feel different without its occupants, but since Harrison King left almost a week ago for work, nothing feels the same.

Leni texted me a bunch of links to posts from excited tourists touting their recent visits to Debajo, plus an article listing it as one of their top hidden gems for the summer.

The next show brought in over twelve hundred partiers.

To celebrate, I took the next day to explore the island, Toro more than happy to show me both tourist places and local haunts.

Natalia, having caught me working at odd hours one too many times, decided I needed a hobby. When I told her about the little crocheted dolls I made during my art school undergrad and sold on Etsy for extra cash, she surprised me the next day with yarn and materials.

If I expected to hear from Harrison about the increase in sales, there's been nothing since the night he came after me like a tuxedo-clad god on the steps of Christian's villa.

"I'm fucking sorry."

As if he expected that to undo everything he'd done.

But the sick thing is part of me wanted to accept his apology. Not only for that night but for all of it.

I start typing out a text to him.

Rae: Toro's started showing me the island by driving me around, but I'm pretty sure it's so he can tell stories. Ash broke this blue vase shaped like a mermaid while playing soccer inside yesterday. Barney whines every morning when he sees you're not there.

I pocket the phone without hitting Send.

But later, the thing vibrates in my pocket.

· · ·

Harrison: Tell Toro to take a goddamned day off. Ash needs to fuck around outside. And you can let my dog know I'm catching a flight back today.

Shit.

I must have accidentally hit Send.

There's no dwelling on the humiliation, though, because he's coming back. And I'm looking forward to seeing him.

Instead of my fucked-up feelings over one mysterious billionaire, I focus on this evening's set.

I choose a black jumpsuit, plus the wedge sandals that were returned to me by one of Christian's staff the day after the gala. Once I got over the embarrassment of being tracked down to return the footwear I left in the hall, I decided to break them in.

I like how feminine I feel. Not as much beautiful as powerful.

A goddess, in Harrison's words.

I line my eyes extra dark and take care with my shiny, neutral lip gloss.

"Are you coming tonight?" I ask Ash on my way out.

"I have a date. But it's a secret." He winks.

"Damn secrets. Between you and Harry—"

"Harry?" He cocks a brow. "Have you called him that to his face?"

I glare. "Are you ten years old?"

"Nope, and neither are you." His gaze runs down my body. "Which is why it'll be interesting when he finds out."

Unreal.

"You get why he's more of a prick than usual around you. He's not used to wanting what he can't have. Between you and La Mer...it's a rough summer for him."

As I get into the front seat of the car with Toro, I'm still thinking of Harrison.

I miss his suits. His smooth voice, his icy-blue stare, the firm lips that make my stomach tighten imagining how they'd feel on mine.

How they'd feel other places.

When I get to the club, I drop off coffee and pastries I purchased on the way with security, wave to everyone as I get ready for my set. I even accept a drink to take the edge off.

The crowd goes crazy when I'm introduced and I take over the booth.

Energy flows through me, hot and electric. A power surge of my own creation reflected back at me.

I take it all.

Without thinking, I look up at his private

booth. There's a crowd in suits and cocktail dresses. A dozen men and women are spilling out of the booth and onto the catwalk.

The hairs on my neck lift before I catch sight of his golden head, angular jaw, and square shoulders through the crowd.

Harrison's back.

A surge of emotion rockets through me.

Anticipation, nerves, longing.

I watch as a bartender serves drinks, and they toast.

One woman leans over to whisper in his ear. When her hand lingers on the shoulder of his jacket, I almost fuck up my transition.

But someone nudges my shoulder with a champagne bucket of ice and waters. Plus a bottle of champagne nestled in the middle, a number on a Post-it stuck to the glass.

The door, I realize. Fourteen hundred sixty-three.

It's thrilling. I did this, but it feels like a shared victory. Shared with Leni, the team here, and the man I never thought I'd want to share anything with.

I make a change, dropping in a new song I've been working on. As the chorus comes on, the man I'm totally not watching out of the corner of my eye leans over the railing upstairs.

When I lift my chin and catch him staring, I'm knocked off balance by the expression on his face.

Each beat I feel his eyes on me is a thrill.

A dirty promise that feels less dangerous with the distance between us.

I lift both hands in the air and flip off the catwalk.

A few of the well-dressed people above gasp, but most ignore me.

Harrison King, a decade older than me and probably a dozen tax brackets above, leans elegantly over the railing separating the upstairs VIP booth from the crowd with a glass in one hand.

Then he lifts the other hand and offers me the same finger I gave him.

Good God.

I'm dead. Slain.

If a billionaire flipping me off makes my ovaries flutter, I'm a fucked-up woman.

But it does, and I am, and the smirk on his face is so sexy it makes me throb.

When my set concludes, I drink a gallon of water and take selfies with every fan before I head to the private VIP lounge. Security offers grins and fist bumps along the way.

Leni descends on me the moment I set foot through the door. "You were fucking rad tonight.

Keep doing this, I'll take you on a surfing trip the next time I'm home."

"Deal."

Inside, the room is bustling with twice the usual dozen or so VIPs. Harrison's seated in a booth with a handful of the people from upstairs, perfectly collected in a dark suit that sets off his clear, blue eyes. His legs are stretched out in front of him, women on each side looking as if they'd like to crawl into his lap.

I catch his eye and jerk my head toward the bar.

With a cocked brow, he shifts out of the booth.

"More spoiled princesses?" I ask as he falls into step next to me.

"Business associates."

I feel every inch of him in my space. We're not touching, but having him near is oh so good.

Once we get to the bar, I lean an elbow on it and hold up the sheet of paper from Leni. "Guess what this number is?"

He's close enough I can smell his ocean scent.

"Your SAT score."

I smack his shoulder. "It's the door, dumbass."

Harrison lifts his cool, blue gaze to mine, but the triumph behind it matches the way I feel.

I grin as two drinks are set in front of us. We clink glasses, our arguments set aside for a moment as we share in a victory we've both wanted for different reasons.

"How do you like the espresso machine?" he asks.

"It's very shiny."

His mouth twitches. "I meant, are you pleased with how it functions? It's a new model and the best available."

"I haven't used it."

Harrison frowns, and I take a sip of my drink, feeling his attention linger on me.

Finally, I say, "The French press is good enough. Besides, I don't want to get attached. It's not as if I can take it with me."

"Of course you can. I bought it for you."

"No, I mean... thank you." Processing his confusion is hard. He seems offended his gift didn't rock my world. "But I'm always on the road, so I pack light. The only things that come with me are my computer and gear and clothes."

He leans in, as if genuinely willing himself to understand. "Is it so difficult to see yourself staying somewhere?"

"I've tried that. It didn't work out. People have a habit of disappointing me."

"Perhaps you simply expected too much."

I turn that over as I glance past his shoulder to see his business associates talking and laughing.

"Where were you all week?" I ask.

"Visiting venues in LA and Miami. Putting in place new policies to address a few lingering issues." He hesitates, regret flickering behind his eyes. "In building an empire, it's easy to be lured by the facade and miss the cracks. The past year, I was distracted. I allowed the cracks to extend further than they should."

He was trying to fix the mistakes he made. The ones I called him out for.

I blink.

"I thought your next move was buying La Mer."

"I can do both. You'd be surprised what I can accomplish when I set out to."

It's not the first time he's looked at me as if I have what he wants. But it's the first time I can't resist looking back at him the same way.

The feeling deep in my stomach, expanding in my chest, isn't only attraction. It's not only about how irresistible he looks in his dark suit, how his dirty-blond hair and electric-blue eyes lull me into thinking he could have been the boy next door...

If the boy next door kept a safe full of secrets capable of slicing you clean in two.

"You're an asshole," I whisper, but the warmth in my voice betrays me. "And a prick. And a liar—"

"And you missed me." The gleam in his eye is so sexy it derails my brain.

"I did not."

"Then why did you text?"

"It was an accident." A flush crawls up my face, and his grin widens.

"Ah. But you were thinking of me."

"I'm thinking of how much money I'm going to make in my final two weeks here. But if it helps your ego, *they're* thinking of you." I nod to the fan club across the room.

The women are both pouting their full lips and adjusting their skirts to show even more insanely toned thigh. From the way they're staring, they miss his company.

"My attention is occupied."

I can't stop the surge of adrenaline that pulses through me or the breathless smile that tugs at my lips.

I ask something I know I shouldn't.

"Where do you... you know?"

"What?"

"Hook up. You don't do it at the house. I would've heard you if it was in your room, and I explored every inch of the villa while you were gone. There's no secret sex room or anything."

"Ah. Because I'm such a prolific adorer of women, I must be bedding them indiscriminately? Including since you arrived?"

The flash of his eyes should be a warning.

"Pretty much. I mean, you are the chairman of the British Billionaire Club."

"Excuse me?"

"It's a thing," I go on, deadpan. "You have elections, and meetings, and a dress code. Plus closed door events where you whip out your cash and measure how tall the stacks are."

He leans in and tugs on my hair, his expression solemn. "You're not supposed to know about that."

I toss back my head and laugh. It feels so damn good, and when he grins too, I wonder if it's contagious.

"Besides," he goes on, "I'm keeping busy with the DJ in residence at 'one of Ibiza's hidden gems.'"

He holds out his phone.

I scan the social media post from an influencer who happened to be at one of last week's shows.

His hand covers mine. The contact has my pulse thudding harder as I finish scanning the raving post. "That's fucking awesome," I say.

"It'd be more awesome if she'd clean my pool with her thong."

We made that bargain weeks ago. Something has shifted between us since, though I never gave permission. Now, the alcohol and high from the show and the way he's looking at me have me feeling invincible.

This place might not be my home, but I can't

argue with the feeling pulsing through me, the familiarity of the staff and the setup and the bar, the hope that I could belong here—not only Little Queen, but Rae too.

And the man who owns it, the one I spent months hating, is one I would have run from once but now I want to lean into.

Every time he pushes me, I push back.

I don't break, only bend.

The newfound confidence makes me bold.

"Are you asking?" I taunt.

I'm close enough to see the tiny dots in his shirt print. His body blocks most of the room, and I can only see one of the envious women eyeing us from the corner.

"Come on, Harry, don't be shy. You can admit that what you want most after coming home from a long, hard work trip is a pair of my underwear to jerk off with."

His nostrils flare.

The hit of triumph twines with attraction surging through my veins, a cocktail more potent than the one I'm drinking.

I take the cherry from the bottom of my glass and suck on it.

If I didn't already know I'd raised the stakes, it's evident in the pulse in his neck. The way his gaze darkens with intent as he leans in, resting a hand lightly on my hip.

"Then give them to me."

His rough whisper in my ear, his firm lips tickling my skin, makes me forget basic functions.

Like how to chew.

The cherry gets stuck in my throat, and a second later, he's hitting me on the back. I spit the thing out on the woman crossing the floor to interrupt us. She squeals, flicking the fruit off her dress.

The other occupants of the VIP room fall silent as they stare at us.

Whoops.

Harrison turns to block me from the rest of the room as if I need protection.

Maybe I do.

"Fuck, you're savage." But his mouth twitches.

That's what I get for trying to out-cool this man.

"I can raid my drawer when I get back tonight if you still want a pair of my panties," I say, my voice hoarse.

"No."

"That's what I fig—"

"They don't taste like you. I want the ones you're wearing. The ones you wore when you lifted those middle fingers at my booth."

Desire slams into me, leaving behind a throb of

longing that echoes from the tips of my breasts to between my thighs.

Harrison's jaw flexes as if he knows exactly how his words affect me.

"You can flirt with me, Raegan," he drawls. "I'll even enjoy it. But if you want me to treat you like my equal, you'd better be ready for all that comes with it."

A throat clearing has Harrison wrenching back to look over his shoulder at Leni. "Boss. We need to talk."

He shifts out of his stool, but I swear it's reluctantly. Before he walks away, he says to me, "We're going out tomorrow night."

"Calling in another favor?"

"No. A do-over of the first one. And trust me, you'll want to be there."

13

———

RAE

*I*t started with a picture.

One I posted of the beach when I was out walking Barney one morning.

Since then, I've posted on social nearly every day.

Sometimes with Barney, sometimes the scenery. One day I snapped a photo of Toro, his weathered profile smiling, when he came to work on the house, and we ended up talking for an hour about his daughter and the argument they had about her leaving Spain for a job in Australia with a boy she was dating at the time.

In between, I've reposted pictures from fans. For the first time, my following is growing, and it's people saying they love my shows or my music or want to check out Debajo.

It doesn't hurt that I've been scanning the feeds of some hashtags of local partiers to see what's popular and, more importantly, what people are into but aren't getting in the bright lights and theatrics of the biggest clubs.

It's not Harrison's pressure. It's that I want to make Debajo great. It's less about me, or even getting the money for Callie, and more about believing in a place and the people in it.

This morning, when I check my DMs, the name on top grabs my eye.

Beck, one of my classmates from arts school, who is in LA.

You keep making that party look so good I'm gonna crash it.

I grin. *Don't write checks you can't cash.*

My phone rings as I'm out for a run with Barney. Adrenaline is pumping through my veins as I slow to a walk and answer. After a moment for the video call connection to establish, a handsome grinning face appears.

"I read about you this week," Beck informs me.

"Wow. I didn't know you could read."

His bark of laughter is warm and welcome. Beck's outside too, his hair blowing in the breeze. "Just because I'm an actor doesn't mean I'm stupid."

He's not. My friend took an arts-school vlog

and leveraged it into a TV deal after graduation. He stars as a psychic cop in one of the top shows on television.

"How's the club gig?"

"I'm going to fill the place if it kills me."

"Badass. I heard someone's birthday's coming up from Tyler and Annie. Which day is the party?"

I frown. I haven't talked to Annie in a couple weeks except for the odd text. "There's no party, Beck. My birthday's not a day to remember."

He cocks his head, surprised. "Clearly you need to replace it with better memories."

"I'm trying. Tonight, I'm going to the biggest club on the island."

When I woke up an hour ago, there was a note on my dresser in Harrison's scrawl saying we were going to La Mer to scope it out.

Excitement bubbled through me when I stared at it, then the bottle of pills I had demoted to the dresser from my bedside table earlier in the week and replaced with a tiny vase of fresh flowers from Natalia's garden.

"Sounds like fun."

"It's recon," I say.

"Even better."

Tonight, I dress for the occasion. A cropped white top. A skirt that shows off my legs. The platform wedges Harrison got me. I try my hair a few different ways before twisting it up into buns on my head.

I look like a warrior, and maybe I am one.

It doesn't feel as if Harrison and I are on opposite sides since he went on the trip to clean up his clubs in person.

Tonight, we both want the same thing.

La Mer.

"Come on, Rae," Ash hollers from the other side of my door.

"Bossy, considering I invited you," I call back.

Harrison had frowned over his coffee when I informed him I'd called his brother, but he'll get over it.

If I'm being honest, it feels safer to have Ash there.

The door opens without my permission, and Ash surveys me.

"Jesus," the younger King says before I can protest.

I plant a hand on my hip. "Good Jesus or bad Jesus?"

"There's one Jesus," Ash says solemnly. "And he's always good."

I laugh as I follow him downstairs. "Wait. Where's your brother?"

"He said he'd meet us there. And it's a good thing because if he walked in on you looking like this, I'd be going to La Mer alone."

I glance down at my outfit. It's more skin than I'd normally show but nothing compared to some of the outfits that grace Ibiza's clubs every night, including Debajo.

"It's just me, Ash."

"You don't understand. When Harry sees something he wants, it's game over. He's trying to stay away, but the fact that he can't have you is killing him."

As thrilling as it feels to be the object of Harrison's interest, we can't pursue it. Giving in to him feels like giving in to something bigger. A man like that casts a long shadow, and it's only beginning to feel as if I'm getting myself back after the hellish year I've had.

I won't risk losing myself in him.

Even for a night I've found myself fantasizing about more than once.

"Do you think he'll ever trust someone again?" I hear myself ask. "After Eva, I mean."

"I hope so."

Toro drives us to the club, checking on us from the front with eyes crinkling at the corners. When we pull up, the door opens from the outside, and a hand extends to take mine.

I shift out of the car and look up.

My heart stops.

Harrison King is breathtaking in chino shorts and a midnight-blue linen shirt, and I press my lips together as he surveys me.

"You dressed down," I say.

"A necessary evil to be inconspicuous. You, on the other hand, barely dressed at all."

"I thought you'd like it."

"You wore this for me?" His eyes warm with hunger.

"That's a big leap from 'I thought you'd like it'."

"It's a logical inference. And I do like it. Very much."

His attention pins me in place for a heartbeat, two, before the passing crowd makes me notice the doors of the club are around the corner.

"I asked Toro to drop you beyond where we might be spotted," Harrison supplies, refocusing on our surroundings.

"And I told the guys from the club I'd meet them inside," Ash adds.

"Why do you want this club so badly?" I ask Harrison as I take careful steps along the sidewalk, sneaking another look at him. I've seen him in a tux, a suit, and almost naked. The casual clothes might be my favorite.

"La Mer would be the crown jewel in my collection."

I groan. "What is it with you Brits and your crown jewels?"

He ignores me. "Mischa wants it. I want to take it away from him."

"All because of what happened with your parents?"

"Yes."

"No," Ash says at the same time, glancing over his shoulder. "Don't pretend it didn't start sooner." His gaze drops to Harrison's chest so fast I almost miss it.

"Mischa has a reputation," Harrison says. "People who disagree with him get silenced."

"So, you're the good guy."

He frowns. "Let's say it's good you called me out on my club's security and not Mischa's, or we wouldn't be here talking."

The idea of a person more fucked up than Harrison, someone who'd stop at nothing to get what he wants, is enough to make me shiver.

We approach the end of the huge line, and I reach for my wallet. "I have Christian's card."

Harrison tucks it back in my bag, tugging me

by the elbow toward a back door. "We're not letting Christian know we're here."

At the door, Harrison shakes hands with a security guy who lets us inside. Ash leading the way, Harrison at my side with his hand on my back, we head through a dark tunnel, only the music at the other end guiding us.

"So did you fuck your hand to my new song after Debajo last night?" I ask conversationally.

His arm flexes around my waist. "Did you lie awake all night thinking about it?"

I catch a toe on the ground and nearly trip.

The idea of Harrison King thinking of me while he unfastens his dress pants and shoves down the zipper is insanely sexy. His heavy breathing, roughened with pleasure and anticipation as he stroked the hard length of his cock. The flex of his muscles, the way he'd seek out his own brutal pulls as he cursed me.

I wonder how it would feel to wrap my hand around him and watch his eyes narrow to slits. To reduce him to curses, then no words at all.

Too soon, we're in the open-air club, and the impossible tension slips a few notches.

I'm awestruck by my surroundings. It's an ode to the stars. A spectacular amphitheater built for revellers.

The crowd is young and beautiful and ready

for the release this place promises.

"If you buy it, you'll need the best DJs," I comment, breathless.

"I'm not concerned. It's not only the crowd that lines up for this place."

"I've wanted to play here forever," I admit, soaking it all in. "To hear my songs, to feel them through the ground, like they're moving the earth." I cut him a teasing look. "If you buy it, you'll let me play, right?"

"La Mer is the biggest stage in the world." His brows lift, and I feel my smile fade.

Hurt slices at me, cutting deeper than I thought this man could cut me.

"And you don't think I'm good enough."

He was by my side as I breathed new life into his club, and despite his sparse praise, it felt as if he was cheering me on. That we were in this journey together.

Harrison shakes his head as if I'm being unreasonable. "I didn't say that."

"Yeah, you did." I twist away from his grip and slip into the throng of people.

Watching the booth, envy settles into my gut like a throbbing mass. The man spinning tonight is Maxx, a DJ I met at Coachella. He has a reputation for being a dick to new talent, especially women.

The thing is he's not alone. Of Billboard's top

one hundred DJs in the world, only a handful are women. None of the top ten.

I want to make that list, not only because that list determines who gets booked and who makes bank.

Women have always been involved in music, but when it comes to recognition and compensation, it's still a man's world.

I try to forget the hurt and dance with Ash and his friends while Harrison's off doing whatever he has planned.

A guy from Ash's crew brushes up behind me. He's fit and attractive, but when he moves closer, reaching out to draw me against him, I pull back. "I can't."

He shrugs and returns to dancing.

I'm in the middle of the biggest club in the world, crushed because a rich, entitled man I have no reason to care for doesn't believe in me.

It's not possible to hate someone and like them at the same time.

Is it?

The next time the song transitions, everything changes.

The first chords are familiar.

I feel them in my body before I hear them.

I spin and latch onto Ash, who's dancing with a few other guys, by the front of his shirt.

"Was this you?" I demand, but Ash shakes his head.

I stumble back, searching for Harrison. Pushing through the crowd, I scan the sea of faces and bodies. It's an impossible throng, but I wade through anyway, tripping over my shoes until strong arms grab me at the edge of the dance floor.

I look up to find Harrison King looming over me, cool and breathtakingly beautiful.

"It's my song," I shout, my heart thudding against my ribs.

I squeeze my eyes closed, imagining me playing this song from the stage.

As much as I've grown to care about Debajo, mixing at La Mer would make my career. Hearing my song in the place cements the possibility that it can happen.

That it *will*.

When I blink my eyes open again, he's closer than before. He smells like man and the ocean.

His hands find my waist when I threaten to tip over from the giddiness.

I straighten with his help, his face inches from mine.

Those eyes are hot, his mouth parted.

I'm at the world's biggest party, and all I see is Harrison, filling my vision.

"This was you," I accuse. My fingertips dig into

his corded biceps, the tense muscles holding me up.

"You fucking—"

He shuts me up with his mouth.

His lips claim mine, rough and impatient and a little bit desperate.

He's warm and hard, delicious and sharp. His heat and scent wrap around me.

It's less like kissing than an attack, but an unplanned one by a skilled fighter.

The feel of him has me tingling, every nerve ending alive and throbbing. His hard body is pressed to mine, his heart hammering faster than the beat surrounding us—the one I made myself.

The hardness grinding against my stomach would steal my breath if his kiss hadn't already.

The music pulses around us, the crowd throbbing.

I'm throbbing.

What he says about power is true—I feel his, and it's pure temptation even before his touch strokes up my thighs, his hand gripping my ass to fit me against him.

My spinning head can't tell if it's seconds or minutes later when he pulls back an inch, eyes dark as the sky.

"You're welcome," he whispers against my mouth.

14

HARRISON

I'll never admit it to anyone, but sometimes I'm a fucking idiot.

Still, I'm never a fucking idiot two days in a row.

I rise early and punish my body with a hard workout before showering and selecting a suit. It's nearly ten when I meet Toro at the front of the villa for the drive to Christian's house.

"Pleasant evening?" he asks, meeting my gaze in the mirror.

"Interesting."

Getting Rae's song played last night at La Mer wasn't planned.

I believe in her, but I'm practical too. The business part of my brain reminded me La Mer has its pick of the world's top DJs regardless of who owns it.

And she will be one of the best.

The possibility that she needed to hear that had never occurred to me because she's so damn independent.

I'm supposed to want to put things right in my business, and my life. It matters more than anything. Except...

All I could think about last night was proving myself to Rae.

So, I grabbed her and did what I've been thinking about for fucking weeks.

Kissing her on the dance floor wasn't planned, but when I saw her cutting through the crowd, searching me out, a beast unfurled inside me. One that wanted to protect her. To make sure nothing ever hurt her the way I had.

My reward was the single hottest kiss of my life.

She's infiltrated my life, and I have no one to blame but myself. I brought her here, was hellbent on punishing her and reclaiming what she'd cost me.

Instead, she's turned me inside out.

She's a siren with a sound system and the power to move everyone she can reach. And even though she hasn't spilled her problems at my feet, I see her pain as plainly as if she had.

The woman lives out of a single suitcase, has a love-hate relationship with the bottle of pills she hasn't touched since I replaced them, and creates extraordinary music.

But I have to keep the part of me that's obsessed with Raegan Madani in check this morning because we're back to business and Brioni.

"Well, if you have more interesting evenings planned, I hope you will celebrate her birthday," Toro says.

"Her birthday?" I echo.

"This weekend."

I bite my tongue before saying what comes to mind. What the fuck do you get the woman you can't get out of your head when you have no business thinking about her?

We're not dating. At worst, she's my hostage. At best, my employee.

Except neither of those labels feels adequate to describe what's happening between us.

I want her in my bed. But more than that, I want to do something for her, something she can't do for herself.

When we pull up to the villa, I shift out of the

car and fasten my jacket, thanking Toro before I take the steps two at a time.

My intention is to conclude this deal today. Of course, the signing will come later, but Christian is a man of his word. He won't reverse once we shake on it.

The door is opened by a young woman with light-brown hair and a familiar bone structure. "Mr. King. Please come in." Her light French accent matches Christian's.

She shows me to a study where the man in question is watching a baseball game.

"Americans. I will never understand them and their sports," he muses.

"But you want to enough to watch a twelve-hour-old Yankees game."

"Don't tell me the winner." He grins. "Perhaps I will need a house there when I retire."

He could buy a dozen. More, if he wanted.

He adds, "My daughter has taken a liking to you."

I glance toward the now-closed doors, remembering the woman who let me in. "That's very flattering."

Christian makes an espresso from the machine in the corner and holds it out. I take the coffee as he makes another.

"As uncivilized as it is, let's be direct," I say. "My interest in the club remains unchanged."

"I'm sure it does." He smirks.

"Your club is unquestionably one of the best. But it is not without weaknesses." I rhyme off a list of things I observed last night, things he must know about.

His smile evaporates, leaving a deep frown.

"All of these things would lower its market value. But I'm prepared to pay full price."

"How gracious of you." His tone drips frost. "Just because you have an idea of what the club needs to be does not mean others share it. You bring it under your empire, it will become a commodity like the others."

"I will not commoditize your venue, Christian. It's a cathedral."

I think of Rae's comments about me being unreasonable and try a new approach. "You knew my parents. You trusted one another, even worked together on a few deals. I'm my father's son, and you can trust me to take care of your legacy."

Christian nods toward two armchairs framing a window, and we each claim one. "On the last point, I agree."

My hands tighten on the overstuffed chair. "So, you'll sell me La Mer."

He takes a sip of his drink—the slowest

fucking sip I've ever seen. "Why don't you show my daughter the city first? After, we can talk."

A dawning sense of horror starts at my toes, creeps up my spine, and finishes on a long inhale. *He wants me to take his daughter out?*

"...finishing her third year of university," he's saying. "Sylvie hasn't spent time here since she was a child."

She still is one.

There are two reasons a woman would want me, and only one of which her father would approve of—my money.

I'm not looking to saddle myself with a charge —even if it means landing the property I've coveted for as long as I can remember.

My refusal has nothing to do with the face of another woman occupying altogether too much space in my brain. One who's also too young for me but who elicits an entirely different reaction at the thought of being saddled with her.

I choose my next words carefully. "I'm a terrible tour guide. And I'm quite sure I have nothing else to offer your daughter."

"Are you seeing someone?"

"Perhaps the woman you brought to my party?" Christian presses. "She was charming."

I gesture toward the television. "An American on holiday."

"Ahh. She'll go back to her world, and you'll be in yours."

The truth in his words makes me want to break the espresso cup.

She's back with a vengeance. The way she looks playing the booth at my club. How she flips both fingers in the air.

How I want her not to sheathe her claws but bare them, to rake them over every inch of me.

I hate the idea of her leaving. Once I arrange the purchase of La Mer, I'll finish the season in Ibiza and return to... what exactly? Shuttling between properties in London and Tokyo? Eating expensive meals with socialites and models, doing deals on airplanes?

Even if I wanted to get closer to Rae, her contract is almost up. She'll be gone with the money she so shrewdly bargained for, and I'll have a resurrected club in the form of Debajo.

It seems a fair trade.

But it doesn't feel like it.

"Harrison, I would like to finalize this deal as much as you would. I'm an old man with many things occupying my time until I can divest myself of them. However, I can't focus on them when the most important one is beyond those doors." He gestures toward the hallway, his eyes crinkling. "I'm asking you, as a friend, to take my daughter around town. She hasn't told me she wants this, but I sense it in her. She would not ask for it. And alas, she does not want to be shown by her father."

I set the espresso on the table, untouched.

"As long as you and she understand this is nothing more."

He lifts his hands. "I would not presume to meddle in matters of the heart. I am more interested in matters of finance." Christian drains the last of his coffee before rising, indicating we're done. "And soon, I will no longer be interested in those either."

"Does Toro know you're waxing his car?"

Rae's voice from a few feet behind me later that afternoon makes me straighten from the fender of the Rolls-Royce.

"You wouldn't dare," I say, tossing the rag over my shoulder and wiping an arm across my brow as I turn. "He'll have my head."

In the middle of my driveway, she's a mirage. Her black shorts are trendy, her white top with wide straps that leave her shoulders bare clings to every curve, and her hair is down around her shoulders.

She could pass for a local, and she's stunning.

Rae sidles closer, folding her arms and squinting into the sun to meet my gaze. "He told me he was the first staff you hired back after your parents died once you could afford to."

"A man needs a driver and a housekeeper."

"Did you have a house to keep?"

"A rental at first," I concede, returning to my task.

"I didn't know you owned a T-shirt."

"Only this one." If I'd known a T-shirt would have this effect on her, maybe I would wear them more often. "When I need to clear my head, I try to do something... simple."

I'm still bothered by my meeting with Christian and not comfortable with where we landed. Part of my discomfort has to do with the woman next to me.

Rae surveys the car and me. "Well, your head doesn't seem clear, and the car's shinier than the day it came out of the factory."

I arch a brow. "Meaning?"

"Meaning let's go."

Twenty minutes later, we're at the docks in town, walking amongst the tourists and those who've docked their yachts.

She told me to wear the T-shirt and shorts, but I changed into a short-sleeved button-down.

I might be grumpy, but I'm not a heathen.

Rae frowns at the yachts. "These boats are ridiculous."

Her surprise makes me grin. "It's Ibiza. The owners come here to play and to show off."

I nod toward the nearest vessel. "The *Ariadne*. She's here every summer."

"What about that one? *Dolce Vita*."

"Usually not until later in the year."

My phone buzzes, and I frown, holding it away to read the screen.

"You do need glasses," Rae murmurs, and I scoff.

"A sign of weakness."

"A sign you're smart enough to know you can't fucking see." Her plain tone makes me press my lips together. "And I think they'd look good on you."

I pocket the phone, conflicted. A single word of praise from this woman turns me into a damn teenager.

"You've never been on one?" I nod at the yachts. "They have all manner of toys. Saunas, pool, theaters, private chefs."

"Because there's nothing like a meal from your private chef on a boat like that." Her voice is dry, but there's a hint of curiosity under the surface, as if she wants to know for sure.

"There's nothing like fucking on a boat like

that. Conquering the ocean, feeling as if nature herself can't help but tremble along with the person beneath you."

She turns toward me, and the expression on her face has my body heating in arousal as I think of the kiss last night.

Unplanned.

Disturbingly provocative.

Like her.

"You will play that club someday, Raegan."

She didn't need my belief in her last night, but she wanted it. I've told myself the past few weeks have been about repairing my business, that she was a tool to build Debajo back up to its prior prof-itability.

The fact that I've immensely enjoyed watching her do it is natural. It is my club, after all.

But perhaps it's more than that.

Perhaps it's about *her*.

My words have the opposite effect than the one I intend, making her frown rather than smile.

A group of tourists shoves past us, and I reach out and tug her to my side.

Her curves fit to my body, the ripeness of her breasts, the soft give between her thighs.

We could be any couple on vacation taking a break from devouring one another to enjoy the sights.

Her lips part as she feels how her closeness affects me.

"Ash said something to me—"

"Fuck my brother." I thread my fingers in the hair at the base of her neck, caressing her skin. "It's not my brother you get off to. It's not Ash you lay in bed thinking of."

Rae's eyes darken. "Sex doesn't solve problems, Harrison. It creates them."

"Then you haven't had the right partner," I contend.

But when the group has passed, she pulls away.

"You don't have to like me to want me," I say as I fall into step next to her, pretending the rejection doesn't sting.

"I don't sleep with rich, entitled assholes."

I shove both hands in my pockets, hard, and squint into the sun. "Then you'll have to continue to get yourself off."

"Or I'll have to decide you're a good man."

Surprise has me jerking my head to look at her.

"You can be," she goes on. "I've seen it. When you stop being so consumed with conquering the world and you take a moment to appreciate what's in it."

She sweeps her hair off her shoulders, revealing a faint sheen of sweat glistening on her neck.

My next step falters. I'm glad we're not still touching, because she'd feel my heart kick beneath my ribs.

Because I want her body.

But Christ, I might want her approval even more.

"Well, well. What is all this?" Ash calls from the front door.

I jump up from where I'm working on a track on the couch, headphones around my ears.

Ash already has the case open on the dining table, lifting one of the two dozen items inside.

He fumbles it, nearly dropping it on the floor. "Ah, bollocks."

"I thought you were an athlete. What happened to hand-eye coordination?"

"Footballer. Foot-eye coordination. This a new part of your costume?" he asks as I trail a finger over the pairs of glasses.

"They're not for me."

"Ahh." His eyes soften, and I hate how transparent I feel. "You know, the moment you flipped him off at Debajo the first night, I told him if he wasn't going to make a move, I would."

"But you haven't," I point out, pushing the attention back onto him. "It's never been like that with us, even at the start."

He frowns at the lenses in his hands, but I press.

"What is your type, Ash?"

Before he can answer, the door opens and Harrison walks in.

The room gets smaller the instant he steps inside, and it's not because of his size or the tailored suit clinging to every inch of his hard body. It's the way his attention finds me in a heartbeat.

"It's not Ash you lay in bed thinking of while you make yourself come."

The only thing hotter than imagining his filthy mouth on me while I touch myself, the tight-woven sheets smooth on my damp back, is imagining him down the hall *knowing* I'm imagining it.

It's making it harder to remember I'm here to work for him for less than two more weeks.

Three shows, to be exact.

"Hi," he says.

"Hi."

There's a beat of awkward silence before he continues.

"I spoke to Leni about moving your last show. You'll still play Thursday and next Monday, but instead of closing Thursday next week, you'll finish Saturday. I trust that's acceptable to you."

Surprise works through me. He's offering to have me finish on the biggest night of the week. More exposure, and per our deal, more money. I should be irritated he didn't ask me, but there's another aspect of this proposal I'm focused on.

"You want me to stay here two more nights?"

He cocks his head, parsing my response. "Echo will cover any fees to change your travel plans. But you deserve to close on a weekend."

I feel myself nod.

"Well?" Ash slides a pair of glasses onto his nose and turns to face his brother.

Harrison's attention slides to his brother. "You look like a banker."

"Fortunately, I don't need glasses. You do." Ash pulls them off and tosses them at Harrison.

"See? Hand-eye coordination," I mutter as he catches them.

Ash snorts as he heads for the kitchen.

Harrison crosses to me and scans the table. He looks taken aback, as if the designer case sprouted legs and began scuttling over the floor.

"A mix of designers," I say, pressing my fingers together behind my back as self-consciousness kicks in. "I figured you were a 'don't fuck with the classics' kind of guy. Since you won't see an optometrist, they sent options. You can keep the ones you want, send the rest back."

With a moment's hesitation, he slides a pair up his nose and lifts a brow at me.

I'm thoroughly unprepared for how hot he is. Like a barely tamed beast of a man.

"Um, yeah. Those ones."

"I thought he's supposed to be able to read with them," Ash comments helpfully from the kitchen.

I grab my phone and pull up my social media feed, handing it over so Harrison can test the strength of the glasses.

"These seem very effective." But he's no longer looking at the phone as he backs me into the table with slow, deliberate steps.

I'm aware of him and the fact that his brother is a dozen steps away.

"You failed to disclose something important about this weekend," he says softly. I wait for a beat, then two. "It's your birthday."

Dammit. I press both hands to my eyes. "Who do I have to kill?"

"Toro."

"It had to be the old guy with kids." I curse and blink my eyes open as he smirks.

"Don't make plans."

To buy myself an inch of breathing room, I shift up so I'm sitting on the table.

"I'll have to prepare for my final two shows. Especially since one is next Saturday. Besides, I thought you were spending every second convincing Christian to sell you La Mer."

His gaze flickers. "I decided to leave him time to sleep, and eat, and fuck his wife."

"How charitable," I tease.

I realize my mistake immediately as he steps between my knees, forcing my legs apart.

"A man needs a release, Raegan. It's not healthy to work all day without satisfaction at night."

There are mere inches between us, and my heart is racing.

Keeping my voice level is an impossible task. "I don't celebrate my birthday." I lift the glasses from his face, folding them and tucking them into the breast pocket of his jacket. "It's cursed."

He snorts. "How do you figure?"

"It's a long story. And you should be warned... everyone has a birthday. I might get you back on yours."

Blue eyes darken to a flinty gray. "You'd have to stick around."

Surprise has me straightening even as footsteps from upstairs interrupt. Natalia.

Harrison leans across me to close the case of glasses, near enough his scent invades my senses.

"Two extra days is one thing, but I can't imagine staying longer," I murmur, though suddenly I'm wondering what it would be like. "For one, there's the small issue of you hating me."

"I never hated you. I wanted you to fix the damage your words caused."

"You wanted to punish me," I challenge. "I got up in your business and dared to ask questions, and you didn't like it."

His gaze roams my face, then lower. Harrison moves my hair behind my shoulder before wrapping it around his hand like a rope. He tugs on it, forcing my head back, and leans in, his mouth grazing my ear. "I still want to punish you."

His hips press closer, near enough that I feel his hard length between my thighs.

With one jerk of his hands, he could have me on my back.

I want him to.

But when his phone goes off, he shifts away. I resist the urge to wipe my forehead and see if it's damp as the rest of me.

"Don't bother arguing about the birthday," he says when he pockets the device again. "You'll need to pack a couple of bags for our outing."

"I only have one. What kinds of activities are we doing?"

He turns for the door.

"Drinking? Walking? Swimming?" I demand.

"Yes."

I exhale, irritated by the lack of specificity. "Are there sharks?"

He turns back, his heated gaze sweeping my body. "Count on it."

———

I think about those words.

As I try to work on my set for the night, then as I meet up with Leni to talk through new ideas for next weekend.

We hit a high of more than sixteen hundred people, and the bar staff makes me do shots until I trip out of the VIP room high-fiving everyone along the way.

The next day, I head down to a café I like, wearing my wig and sunglasses to meet the interviewer I agreed to see from social media.

The costume helps me feel protected, like this is part of my onstage persona and not edging into my personal life. It reminds me I'm still Little Queen here, not Rae Madani.

"How did you get into producing? You're notoriously tight-lipped about that," she asks when we're seated at a table.

"Just caught the bug as a teenager. Helped when I got a computer and a synth."

"Did your parents buy them for you?"

I flex my hands under the table. "My first one, yeah."

She laughs. "Guess that gave you something to channel your angst. What do they think of your career now?"

Tension climbs up my spine, settles into my shoulders. "We don't talk about it a lot."

"You're one of the only women playing the White Isle this summer. You've stood up for women's rights even when it cost you."

This is why I hate live interviews. It's impossible to filter out these kinds of things. "It's important to speak up for the people who can't protect themselves."

Despite the fact that she's recording, she makes a note. I force myself not to lean over the table to see what she's writing.

"Harrison King is lying low thanks to you," she comments, and the right turn has me straightening. "Have you heard from him?"

It's not common knowledge that Harrison owns Debajo. He doesn't advertise the fact, and she clearly hasn't put it together. I'm not going to do it for her.

"I'd rather focus on the future."

I manage to steer the conversation away from me and toward my music.

As she rises to head to the door, I ask, "When are you expecting to finalize the article?"

"Soon. I'm pulling in more sources, and I'll come by Debajo to take some photos."

"Sure thing. I'm actually closing next Saturday."

There's a wave of nerves as I watch her leave. Playing a show is high stakes, but you get immediate feedback. With the media, you never know what they'll come up with until it's served up to the public on a platter.

I shake myself before dropping back into my seat to review some logistics for the upcoming shows.

Press is good. It'll help Debajo, and my career.

My phone rings immediately after.

"Greetings, cousin. You're unreal," Callie declares.

"Um. Thanks?"

"Truly. With the money you sent, I've been able to cover payroll for another two weeks."

"More will come after the last show," I promise.

"I'll pay you back every cent. I swear."

"You don't need to."

I can almost hear her roll her eyes.

"How's your mysterious, infuriating hottie?"

I turn it over. "Still hot. Still infuriating."

"So, why do you sound as if you've softened?"

"He's planning something for my birthday."

I haven't been able to get details out of Harrison about the birthday outing, though God knows I've been trying.

We've been in tense, flirtatious limbo for the past few days.

I spent extra time on my appearance before my set, hoping he'd be there. He was, and even though he was taking meetings, he spared me a hungry look from upstairs and texted me a song request.

Then we crossed paths when he came downstairs in shorts last night while on the phone. I was grabbing a snack.

"Who're you talking to?" I mouthed.

"China," he mouthed back.

I threw a napkin at him, which he dodged.

Yesterday, he texted me a picture of Barney with a toy in his mouth.

Harrison: ??

. . .

The toy was a crocheted doll a little longer than my hand, with blond yarn hair and a stitched-on frown. It wore a dark-blue costume with a tie.

Thanks to Barney, one of its arms was ripped off.

Rae: Natalia got me some craft supplies the week you were gone.

Harrison: And you were trying to send me a message?

I laughed out loud.

"He sounds romantic." Callie's voice brings me back.

"I guess so," I admit.

Harrison's not the kind of guy looking for an excuse to do something sweet.

If anything, he's the opposite. Determined, single-minded.

The fact that he found out it was my birthday and is making something special from it despite my protests has my stomach flipping like a girl with a crush.

I'm not doodling "Mrs. Harrison King" in my

notebook or anything. I've never pictured myself as the other half of any guy, and he may not even go there again given what happened with his ex.

But the little flutter in my chest feels entirely foreign.

After we finish talking, I respond to some emails and social messages before heading for the door of the café.

The sight through the glass makes me still.

Harrison's strolling down the street as if I conjured him with my mind, looking like elegant sin.

When did I become the girl who has fantasies about a guy in a suit?

But he's not alone. The woman next to him is pretty, with big sunglasses and pale skin under a wide-brimmed hat. She smiles at him as he talks animatedly, gesturing with his hands.

My stomach knots, twisting into a heavy mass.

We're not dating. I'm not looking for a partner, someone to settle down and create one life with, to argue with and compromise with and lie awake at night next to.

No matter what Callie says, I need to keep my feelings for this man in check.

Starting with whatever he has planned for my birthday.

16

RAE

"I feel like a mole," I say.

Blackness surrounds me, but the sun warms the bare skin of my face and shoulders.

"The spy sort? As in *Mission Impossible*?" Ash calls from somewhere ahead.

"No, the underground animal sort. As in I can't see shit."

The wind tugs at my hair, but the cloth around my eyes holds it firm as I walk. It doesn't help that the firm hand on my back is warm and distractingly low.

"Being blindfolded is not my thing," I mutter.

"Then you've never been blindfolded by the right person." Harrison's mouth at my ear sends shivers down my spine.

I'd glare if I could see him. Lucky for him, I can't. "I got up early on my birthday—"

"Eleven," Ash corrects cheerily, sounding farther away.

"To be kidnapped and forced to trek through God knows where." All my attention goes to my other senses—the scent of the sea and the sound of shorebirds. The next step I take, the surface changes, giving and creaking beneath my feet.

"I could carry you," Harrison suggests.

"I'd rather be thrown into the ocean."

"Don't tempt me."

Then the blindfold is gone and light floods my eyes, leaving me blinking in the brightness.

Blocking part of the sun is a huge white boat.

I'm riveted by the monstrosity tethered at the dock.

"You got me a yacht?" My voice rises an octave as I turn to take in Harrison, who's watching intently.

"It's a charter."

"It's a behemoth. A leviathan. This thing blocks out the sun."

Yet it's not the boat but the faces appearing over the edge that take my shock to the next level.

"Hey, birthday girl!" Annie calls. My roommate from performing arts school waves. A big, straw hat protects her pale complexion.

Her husband, Tyler, is next to her, a possessive arm around her shoulders.

Elle, another friend from school, who's now a comedian, holds a bottle of champagne over her head. "Get your ass up here before I drink this all myself."

Ash heads for the boarding ramp, but I turn to stare up at the man by my side.

He's wearing chinos and a dress shirt, his hair ruffling in the barely-there breeze as if even nature can't resist the chance to touch him.

His handsome face is drawn, eyes shielded from the sun with a hand.

I've been to some of the biggest parties in the world, but here, at a private dock with a handful of friends and this man, I'm overwhelmed.

"This is… obscene," I say, struggling to form words.

"You haven't even seen the inside."

I make to grab my bag from him, but he holds it over the water. "You already lost it once," he warns.

"Don't even think about it." I wrench his arm back toward the dock while he smirks.

Even out here, there's an undeniable pull between us.

He sets the bag on the dock and steps closer as

if he's thinking the same thing. But when he reaches up to touch my face, I duck away.

"What is it?" he demands.

"Nothing."

He frowns, unconvinced.

I have a dangerous fascination with a billionaire who buys and sells properties like secondhand synths on Craigslist, and I can't shake the memory of seeing him with another woman as if they were friendly.

More than.

He's around beautiful women all the time for work, but not usually alone, and not looking as relaxed as he did strolling through the streets.

It's not as if I have a right to him. I can't blame him for spending time with another woman.

But what does throw me is how it felt.

Like the fluttering in my stomach was quashed with a baseball bat.

I turn away from his scrutiny, and as soon as I step onto the deck, Annie wraps me in both arms and squeezes hard.

I shove any other thoughts from my mind as I pull back to stare at her stomach.

"You're huge." I glare accusingly at Tyler, who only lifts a shoulder.

It makes sense the rock star gets along with Harrison. They have the same serious, distant vibe.

Annie, by contrast, is warm and genuine as she leans in. "You want a play-by-play on how the pregnancy thing went down?"

"Not as long as you guys are good. Hey, E, thanks for coming. You guys know Harry. Harrison," I amend, flicking him a look as he responds only with a raised eyebrow. "This is his brother, Ash."

They exchange greetings.

"Welcome aboard." The captain introduces himself with a smile, gesturing to two waitstaff. "We're here to provide for your every need. We'll be heading to Formentera shortly, which is only a short trip away. I expect you'll want to take a look around. But first, would you like something to drink?"

"Yes to the drinks," Elle decides. "Aren't we short a person?"

Annie holds up her phone. "Beck called. He's running late."

Ash checks his watch in irritation. "We'll miss our chance to go snorkelling. You don't want to spend your birthday at the docks, do you?"

"Let's wait for him and take a look around," I decide.

The sundeck has sun loungers at one end, plus its own dip pool. There's a huge dining area with a table set for six that could easily seat double. We head belowdecks next, and it's even more insane.

"There's a sauna and steam room. Plus, a screening room," Harrison says.

He shows us the theater, and Elle sucks in a breath in admiration.

"Six cabins. Choose whichever you like." He gestures to the doors along a small hallway. "Except the master suite."

My friends chatter about the space, but Harrison's loaded stare locks with mine.

Does he think we'll room together? Is he planning to seduce me this weekend with the boat and the big gesture?

As conflicted as I am by what I saw yesterday, the idea of him and me, nothing between us but a giant bed to muffle our sounds, makes my body ache.

I'm empty in a way I wish was only physical.

He's older. Experienced. He's probably had a ton of sexual partners, and it shouldn't matter if he has.

But there's nothing casual about the way I feel. I want him, but not if I'm wondering whether he's comparing me to someone else he's sleeping with... or planning to once I leave.

"There're two jet skis, plus a small fishing boat.

A million other toys also," Ash is saying as we finally head back upstairs.

"How big is this?" Annie asks as the staff bring our drinks.

"Forty-five meters," Harrison says.

"Ridiculous."

"It's just big enough," comes a voice from behind me.

I turn to see a handsome man step onto the sundeck. His dark hair is swept up by the breeze, his eyes shielded by designer glasses. The only other thing he's wearing is swim trunks, his shirt hanging from the back, revealing a torso and arms even more toned than the last time I saw him.

"Beck." The grin that tugs across my face is genuine.

"Good thing you got the big boat. My ego has grown." He crosses to me and sweeps me up.

"Impossible." I wheeze around his thick forearms digging into my ribs.

Beck finally sets me down. "Happy birthday, Little Queen. You look good."

"You look like a Hollywood douche." My gaze drops to his toned stomach. "Shit. Did you buy an ab roller?"

Beck chuckles, nodding to the waitstaff for a drink. "Yeah right. I have a trainer who makes more an hour than I used to pay in rent."

I catch Harrison staring.

"Why are we mov—oh!" I suck in a breath as the engines kick in and the yacht pulls away from its mooring.

Beck hands me a towel, and I lay it on one of the lounger-style seats facing my friends. Harrison takes my bag toward the doorway that goes belowdecks.

"Where are you going?" I call.

"Taking your bag to your cabin. Given how protective you are of it, I wouldn't leave it to the staff."

I trot over to him. "I need to get something," I murmur, bending to unzip my bag.

He waits while I open it and riffle through for sunscreen.

A scrap of black lace falls out onto the deck, and he picks up the panties with one finger. "Care to explain?"

My heart stops. I grab the panties out of his hand and stuff them back into the bag. "They're called underwear."

"Lace," he corrects.

"A woman can wear lingerie for herself."

"But you don't. You wear T-shirts and cotton knickers."

My jaw drops, and he cocks his head.

"No, I think this means you've decided you respect me. Or you did, before today."

I shield my eyes, staring up into his gorgeous face.

I want his hard mouth on mine, those strong hands touching me. But if we do that, I want to know I'm what *he* wants.

Even it's only for a night.

"You can't buy me with a boat," I murmur.

"Wasn't trying to." Harrison leans closer, smooth and determined.

He stops when our lips are an inch apart, not meeting. I suck in a breath that's salt air and him.

"I know you're young," he says. "I'm giving you space because it's your birthday. But whatever shit thoughts have been going through your head? I promise they don't change what's between you and me."

The next second, he's belowdecks, my bag in hand, and I stare after him until my friends call my name.

17

———

HARRISON

*W*hen the yacht docks at Formentera, I'm still in the master cabin taking steadying breaths and willing my gut to unknot.

This day hasn't gone the way I planned. Rae was supposed to see the yacht and her friends and fall at my feet.

I've never met a woman who wasn't swayed by a gift either expensive or heartfelt. This one was fucking both. Yet before getting on this ship, she looked at me as if she would rather spend this weekend with anyone else.

Even though the chemistry between us scorches hot enough to burn through the shiny white hull of this boat.

The vibration of my phone on the bed next to me does nothing to calm my restlessness.

"What?" I bark into the speaker.

"How's your weekend away?" Leni asks.

I inhale, straightening to stare in the mirror across from the bed. "Not as advertised."

"Christian wants to invite you for a private dinner. Apparently, he lost your cell number, so he called me at the club."

The time I spent with Christian's daughter yesterday, playing attentive host to her flirtations, only reinforced that I'm not interested in a pretty young face. Once, I would've entertained such a flirtation. A few dates, some lingering looks, and she would've been telling her father to give me the club for free.

Now, I have no appetite to play the game. It feels not only tired and pointless but wrong. Since when did I start caring about people I barely know?

"He told me to tell you he's inviting Mischa too."

Leni's words cut through the haze in my brain.

No. I'm not playing games, but the old man is.

"There's something else," she presses. "The LA club you went to visit? There was a hiccup early this morning. An incident."

The face looking back at me in the mirror grows still. "What kind of incident?"

"A woman claims she was assaulted."

I switch to speakerphone so I can pull up my email. There are dozens of messages, which is to be expected, but there's nothing from my LA club.

"Where was security?" I snap.

"Not by another client. By a staff member."

Christ.

The room is too small. I yank open the door and take the stairs to the top and step into the bright daylight. I feel in my pocket for my sunglasses and find only the reading glasses Rae got me.

I stare at them a moment before setting them carefully on a nearby table. "I was just in LA last week dealing with this. We cleaned house. Agreed on new policies."

"With the number of clubs you have, there are bound to be problems. But this is shitty timing. She hasn't spoken to the media yet. But there's a possible lawsuit and obviously the PR issue if this gets out."

My mind races. "Is the woman hurt?"

"She's fine. But it would really help all of your venues to have the good press right now."

"What are you suggesting?"

"You're spending a lot of time with the same DJ who accused you this spring. If she went on the record saying she's seen what you're doing and supports you, that could go a long way."

The sounds of laughter from below us draw me to the railing around the anchored boat. I squint into the shadows to see Rae, Ash, and the others playing in the water twenty feet away. Her black bathing suit shows off every curve of her body. Curves I could be touching, or at least experiencing up close, if I wasn't up here.

Rae had something on her mind this morning when we arrived. I wish I could get her alone and force the truth out of her.

I drag my attention back to the call and grip the phone tighter. "She's already playing my club."

"And no one has made the link publicly. Yet."

"It's not happening, Leni."

"Because you have feelings for her?"

I exhale heavily.

"DJs would kill to play a club in Ibiza for a month," she points out. "You've given her an opportunity—one she can use to not only get back to where she was but take her career to the next level. If she has feelings for you too, maybe you could help each other."

"Is this guy for real?" Ash demands from the row ahead of us in the theater room, nodding toward Beck.

Tyler and Annie are huddled together at the front. Elle's in the second row, along with my brother and Beck. We're here to watch Beck's screening copy of the pilot for his new reality show.

I waited for Rae to head into the back row, then I gave her zero outs as I shifted in after her.

From the moment we started watching, half my attention was on the antics of the guy on screen and the rest was on the woman beside me.

"How was Formentera?" I ask under my breath.

"Fun. But you missed it."

I extend my legs in front of us. "Business came up."

I feel her turn toward me. "Why do all this if you weren't going to participate?"

"Because you deserve it."

She turns that over. Her black shorts and sleeveless top leave her long, curvy limbs on display. Her hair, swept up in two piles on top of her head, makes my fingers itch.

"No one deserves to rent a forty-five-meter boat," she decides.

My lips twitch. "*Charter.*"

I think about Leni's suggestion that we could use Rae to get good press. To show the world Echo Entertainment is moving in the right direction. A month ago, she wouldn't have considered it. But now...

"Look!" Beck calls, leaning over the front row of seats. "Remember the releases you signed for this clip from your wedding party in LA? We used the footage."

Annie and Rae are in the background, and as the video captures Beck's speech, Rae stiffens next to me.

"What is it?" I ask, instantly on alert.

"At the party, I had bruises on my wrists. A fan got past security the night I played your club and grabbed me."

Every muscle in my body goes tight, anger simmering up from somewhere deep and dark.

"You told me another woman was hurt," I grind out. "You didn't tell me *you* were hurt."

She returns to watching the screen, but I can't.

Annie laughs in the front row, and Tyler ducks his head to kiss her, making her laugh more.

"I can't promise to have every woman's back," I hear myself say. "But I will do my utmost to ensure that never happens in my clubs again. And I will damned well have yours."

Rae stiffens for a moment, then relaxes.

I rest my thumb and forefinger at the back of her neck, pressing lightly through the rest of the show.

RAE

Dinner is chef-prepared and exquisite, and I wish I could enjoy it fully.

From the head of the table, barefoot in chinos and a white shirt, Harrison watches me with a protectiveness that's unsettling. But somewhere between the cool evening breeze, the laughter on the air, and his grin when he brings out the cake, I can't hate it.

Beck insists on feeding me cake, and I don't realize until I'm laughing through a delicious bite that Harrison has gone still.

Annie groans, bracing an arm on the railing as we sit on the lounging deck after dessert. "That was better than sex."

"I came at least twice just from the cake." Elle rubs her stomach.

"Where's the testosterone?" Ash appears from belowdecks, his hair blowing in the night breeze.

"Drinking at the other end of the boat."

Ash's smile vanishes as he cranes his neck that way. "Hollywood too?"

I shift forward. "You don't like Beck."

"The guy made us watch his home movie," he gripes.

"Come on. It was a screener of his TV show. That's a little different."

Ash waves it off. "He's the self-indulgent type who does anything for attention. Trust me, I've met lots of them over the years at private school and in sports."

"Well, you're missing out," Annie says. "They're drinking a new line of bourbon I brought from my dad's company."

"Jax Jamieson's personal collection?" Ash rubs a hand over his jaw. Annie's dad is an even bigger rock star than her husband, though he's semi-retired from the stage to raise two kids with Annie's stepmom in Dallas while working on his own label. "Fuck, I can't pass that up."

Ash walks in the direction of the other guys, and a moment later, the deck is quiet.

"Just us girls," Annie murmurs.

I cut her a look. "Time to paint each other's toenails?"

"Let's play 'Never Have I Ever,'" Elle decides as the waitstaff comes to top up our champagne.

"Annie's not drinking."

"That means I'll win." Annie winks.

Elle starts. "Never have I ever... fucked a musician."

Annie and I both drink.

"Careful of all those bubbles," Elle drawls, and Annie kicks her.

"Really? Not even at Vanier?" Annie asks when she's done.

Our blond friend cackles. "Just because you go to arts school doesn't mean you need to make the rounds of majors. Rae, who was yours?"

"Evan," I recall. "In second year."

"How was it?" Annie leans in.

"He was a yeller. Like, projecting-from-the-diaphragm loud. You'd think the man had conquered a large fishing village instead of my vagina."

The other two crack up.

"Okay, my turn," Annie decides.

"Hey"—I lift my glass—"it's *my* birthday."

"So shut your mouth and enjoy it."

"I am enjoying it," I admit, looking down the boat to where the guys are barely visible at the other end, as decent as they are handsome. We spent the afternoon on the beach, had an incredible dinner and dessert. I'm so happy it hurts. "I can't believe you came all this way to see me."

"Yeah, the scenery's crap," Elle supplies, and Annie slaps her arm.

"Mostly we love you," Annie says.

"Your billionaire boy toy made it easy. The plane tickets were delivered to my door," Elle adds.

"Yes. About that." Annie straightens. "Tyler and I were a little surprised to get an invitation from Harrison for your birthday. You want to catch us up?"

I turn the glass in my hands, wondering whether its contents or Elle's words are responsible for the sudden tingling in my stomach. "We started out as enemies. Now I don't know what we are. I think he's genuinely trying to improve his clubs, in LA and everywhere else. He had a pretty rough breakup last year, and his ex was part of the reason he lost focus."

"They weren't right for each other?" Annie asks, curious.

"That, plus he doesn't trust easily. He's not the kind of guy to put a relationship ahead of everything else he is."

Elle says, "He's doing a hell of a good impression of caring about you."

Her pointed words have that hopeful tingling starting up in my chest again.

Or maybe it's the alcohol. I catch the eye of one of the attendants who tops me up without so much as a word.

Annie takes advantage of my distraction to continue the game. "Never have I ever... slept with someone ten years older."

Elle drinks.

I freeze with my drink halfway to my lips, then lower it again.

"Seriously?" Elle screeches, loud enough to wake whatever bones have settled at the bottom of the ocean beneath us. "He's smart, he's rich, he's the kind of gorgeous that only gets better with age... though I read men reach their sexual peak in their twenties."

She looks to Annie for corroboration, and our friend lifts her hands, surrendering.

"If Tyler gets any better, I might not survive."

I roll my eyes as Elle laughs and says, "Wait. How old is Harrison?"

They both pull out their phones before I can answer.

"He's thirty-five," Elle declares loudly.

"Thirty-five what?" a familiar British voice demands from behind me.

I swallow, shifting on my lounger to stare up at the man in shorts and a linen shirt, the top two buttons open.

"Nothing." It's the most innocent voice I can manage, and it's terrible.

"How old you are," Elle, the traitor, supplies. "Have you read that men's sexual performance declines after their twenties?"

We're joined by Tyler, who sinks onto Annie's lounger and pulls her against him. Beck drops onto Elle's, while Ash's athletic gait carries him to the edge of the boat, where he leans against the railing.

"Patently false," Harrison replies. "Men in their twenties have physical stamina but no subtlety. Women are intellectual creatures. You need mental stamina to please one."

God, his mouth is beautiful. I want to trace it with my finger.

Then shove it between my thighs.

I take another sip of my drink, and the pleasant buzzing feeling intensifies.

We keep drinking and talking. Tyler shares stories from his tour while Beck presses Ash on his workout routine. Annie talks about pregnancy surprises and their plans to settle in LA once the baby arrives. Even Elle weighs in with cringe-worthy moments from a comedy competition she just finished.

It's fun, until eventually everyone heads to bed.

"I think I'm drunk," I mumble as strong arms carry me down the stairs.

"Indeed," the person carrying me agrees, the word vibrating through his body and mine.

I scrunch up my nose. "What language are you even speaking?"

"That would be English."

"That wood bee ingleesh," I parrot.

I'm deposited on a soft surface, and I sigh as I force my eyes open.

Harrison's over me, his shirt unbuttoned enough I can see the edge of his scars. His hair is sticking up, his expression amused and more relaxed than I've ever seen it.

I'm so enchanted that it takes a moment for me to notice Harrison pull away.

I grab for his arms. "Where are you going?"

"To bed. You're drunk."

I scramble forward onto my knees, a posture I'm sure looks as sexy as it feels. "And if I wasn't? What happened to the big, bad billionaire? The legendary ladies' man?"

He studies me for a moment before his lips brush across my cheek. "Happy birthday."

Anger rises up, along with panic. Maybe I sabotaged this night on purpose, let myself be confused by the big gesture. But I want him. I want this. Tonight.

I shift up onto my knees, grabbing his bare forearms before he can leave.

"No," I protest, knowing in my bleary brain that I'll regret this. "Don't pretend you didn't rent me a boat—"

"Charter."

"—to fuck me on it. There's no other possible reason a man like you would do this for a woman like me."

It's quiet here. No soft lapping of the ocean against the boat. No hum of equipment.

Harrison's gaze lowers to my shoulder, where my bra strap is exposed. "I won't pretend to know what you think a man like me does. But as for a woman like you? There are no women like you. At least as far as I've seen. You arrive at a place with an exit strategy. You look out for people you don't even know, and you demand that others do the same even though God forbid someone look out for you in return. You put yourself on the line every night on that stage, but when you look in the mirror, you don't recognize the girl looking back. It should be too painful to watch, but I can't look away. You are an exquisite train wreck. So, if there's a way a man like me is supposed to treat a woman like you, forgive me. I've never met a woman like you."

Before I can react, the door shuts in my face.

I stare at the ceiling and try to sleep for an hour before stumbling to the bathroom to throw up, brush my teeth, and drink a gallon of water.

Then I stare at the ceiling some more.

We're so damn different. He's older, experienced, at the height of his career while mine is still growing. He's comfortable in his skin while I'm learning how to wear mine. He's a billionaire with a vendetta and enough baggage to sink this yacht, and me...

I have baggage too.

Despite it all, I want him.

The alcohol burns off before my insomnia, so I pull out my computer and headphones and grab a light blanket, carrying all three up the stairs as quietly as I can.

Above deck, night hangs like an indigo blanket. Distant sounds from shore and the soft swish of waves are the only interruption to the silence. In one of the loungers, I open my computer and put on my headphones, opening Ableton Live.

I'm a few minutes into working on a track when movement by the stairs has me stiffening.

An intruder.

Yachts don't have intruders.

Unless there are pirates?

But I recognize the way this pirate moves.

He grips the railing, grimacing.

"Are you sick?" I demand, sitting straight up. "How much did you drink?"

Harrison spins, looking caught out. "Not enough."

I'm barely buzzed now, and my brain is functioning far better since I rid myself of most of the alcohol earlier. "You're seasick. So, why are we on a yacht?"

"Because you wanted it! And I wanted to give it to you."

Oh.

Oh, no.

This larger-than-life, rich, untouchable prick. He wasn't supposed to get me a birthday yacht. Or the cake I like. Or host my friends. Still, he did it all knowing full well he couldn't relax and enjoy himself. That makes my stomach flip in a way that has nothing to do with the slight swaying of the boat.

He braces himself on the railing, a warrior guarding his wound.

But the vulnerability was one he endured on purpose. For me.

I don't know how to respond to that.

But I try.

"My parents split up on my birthday. That's why I hate it." *Part of it, anyway.*

"How old were you?"

"Sixteen." The muscles in my chest and stomach knot. "But high school was pretty shit even before that."

I lean over the railing a few paces down from him.

"You want to tell me about it?"

The lights of the harbor are visible from where we're anchored. Ibiza looks like a fairy island.

But I only half see it, remembering how many birthdays passed without the friendship and love I felt on this one. How many other days, too.

I shake my head. "Today was good. I don't want to mess with it."

He's silent a long time. "I'm not trying to diminish what you experienced. But if you ever think you're damaged, or broken, or less of yourself because of what happened in those years... you're not."

The backs of my eyes burn.

I don't talk about my life with men. Not my life before or now. Hell, I don't talk about it with my friends.

Letting him in makes the distance between us feel smaller. I shouldn't want that, but sometimes I think I'm drifting.

A boat without an anchor.

"You asked me why things were weird between

us earlier," I start. "I saw you in the city with a woman yesterday."

He shifts off the railing, crossing to me. "You were jealous."

"It threw me," I correct when he stops close enough that when I breathe in, I can't tell him from the ocean.

His eyes dance, his hair lifting in the breeze as his tight lips curve. "You were jealous."

I exhale an exasperated breath. How is he amused by this?

"Stop—"

"You were jealous. Say it."

"Why? So you can tell me I can't have you? Trust me, I've already told myself enough times."

His eyes flare with heat before he banks it again. "She's Christian's daughter. He asked me to take her around town as a favor."

He lets that sink in before continuing.

"The only woman on my mind is a brat who plays in my club. Lives in my house. Is altogether too distracting."

His confession cuts my protests off at the knees.

My gaze drags down to his shirt hanging open to reveal his firm pecs and abs.

I trace the shape of the scars on his chest with a finger, brushing his shirt back so I can.

"Tell me what happened?"

It's a request, not a command. And when I meet his gaze, I have the feeling he'd tell me anything I wanted.

"Mischa."

My stomach twists, and it's not from the alcohol. "He did this to you? You told me it was at boarding school."

Everyone's teenage years are fucked up.

He nods. "There's a tradition when you win head boy, you get marked by the boy who lost to you. It's a sign of mutual respect. Teachers don't condone it, but they tolerate it. There was only one time in our school's history it got bad and a kid almost bled out."

My eyes widen.

He says, "Usually it's a letter. A few shallow scores with a pocketknife."

"Yours is a crown."

"Thirteen cuts. Prick fancied himself an artist. Took four days for him to complete it," he says, grimacing.

"You didn't complain?"

"No. Nearly passed out once, but I didn't say a fucking word."

"You've hated him since you were a boy."

"He's hated me," Harrison corrects. "Since my parents left his parents' business. They told

Mischa to convince me to work for them, to be groomed for the same position my parents held. I turned him down in no uncertain terms. They weren't happy with him, and he's hated me since. It's why he was so intent on taking Eva from me. Now, I want to finish him. Put it behind us once and for all. La Mer is the nail in the coffin."

The world of buying and selling businesses like they're moves on a chessboard feels so far beyond me. But at the same time, it's not.

Because what they're chasing isn't the money.

It's the feeling.

The feeling of being right. Justified.

Of laying your head on the pillow at night and being satisfied you did the best you could.

"She's missing out," I murmur.

He laughs. "Trust me, if Eva wants a yacht, he'll get her one."

"Wasn't talking about the yacht."

I press my hand over his heart.

His lashes tremble as his gaze searches mine in the dark.

I can't deny how I feel anymore. It's not only attraction. I care about him, whether I have any business caring or not.

I want to distract him from his sadness, the effects of the sea beneath us. "Come on. Let me show you what I'm working on for my final show."

He shifts onto the lounger and sits behind me. I move between his legs and tug the blanket over both of us. His hard thighs wrap around me, making it impossible to focus entirely on my computer.

"I've had this melody I can't get out of my head." I shift a few clips around, frowning. "There's an easy kick for now—I'll figure out the rest of the drum structure later—but I'm working on the frequency. I want to drop the frequency down on this part"—I point at the screen—"probably eighty hertz, close to sub. You don't really hear it anymore, but you feel it."

After making the adjustment, I hit a keystroke to play the phrase again.

Harry tugs me back against him. "How do you know what to change?"

"Experience. Intuition. Fucking it up enough times." I tilt my head up to grin at him, and the expression on his face hits me square in the chest.

His scent is like the ocean surrounding us— mysterious, undeniable, overwhelming.

"Sounds like running a business." His voice is full of humor as he strokes my arm lightly.

"I can change frequencies to change the feel of something too."

When I lift my arm, his touch lands on my side.

I suck in a breath. It's more intimate now.

Instead of hesitating, he strokes down farther.

"Every amateur with a computer thinks he can make music," I quip, but when his fingers slip down my stomach, I have to swallow my groan.

His breath is warm on my temple. "I could."

"Oh really? You're a prodigy?" It's a joke, but when the loop starts again on my computer, his fingers move with it.

I bite my lip as I try to focus, but his touch is lighting fires between my thighs. He nudges the waistband of my shorts, revealing the edge of dark lace beneath.

His exhale is hunger and satisfaction at once as he strokes a finger where my panties meet my skin.

"Did I mention I like these?" The low pitch of his voice is pure seduction.

"You might've hinted at it."

My heart thuds harder, all from the slow touch of his fingers. From knowing he's looking at the lace I put on. Knowing I put it on for him.

"I've watched you give in when you play, but I never see you give in anywhere else. I want to see it." Harrison's chest vibrates under me. "I want to feel it."

His touch slips lower, where I'm already wet.

I arch up off the lounger, but his other arm bands around me to hold me to his chest, the impressive hardness probing my lower back.

I'm a knot of pure need, every part of me reduced to the spot where his fingers touch me. The connection feeds the part of me starved for attention, affection.

"Oh my God," I mumble.

It's the most exquisite feeling. He knows what he's doing to me. It's deliberate and every bit as sexy as his shallow hiss of breath at my ear.

I want to turn over and look in those cool, blue eyes, see if they're shattered with heat. I want to kiss him, to press every inch of me against him, to feel as if we're coming together and I'm not at a disadvantage anymore. But I'm trapped between his hands and body, and when I move an inch, the computer slips.

I grab for it.

This was supposed to be a demonstration.

I try to refocus on what I was saying, but his finger moves lower, sliding through my wetness, and I inhale sharply.

"I've never understood why a producer invests so much time getting the parameters just right," he murmurs. "Humans can handle limited sensory input. Like right now, you can feel my breath on the side of your face. But when I do this..." Harrison adds the heel of his hand to the mix, rubbing against my swollen clit. It's dissonant and raw and euphoric at once.

"You lose track of everything except where I'm touching you." His rasp in my ear makes me clench, aching to have him fill me.

It's not the kind of safe pleasure I give myself. It's strange and overpowering.

My nails dig into his thigh, and when he slips a finger lower still, teasing my entrance, I shiver.

"Tell me how it feels."

"Big," I confess.

I meant the feelings, not his finger, though that is too, but he chuckles softly.

"Beautiful girl. If this is big, you have no idea what you're in for."

The insistent outline pressing me from behind is a reminder he's right.

"You'll have to pace yourself. You're not in your twenties anymore," I chide, reminding him of the conversation earlier.

His groan is full of promise. "You're fucking right I'm not. The things I'll show you."

My blood heats more, and even the ocean breeze isn't enough to cool my damp forehead. "You think you can teach me about sex?"

"No. I think I can teach you about yourself."

He adds another finger to the first, pressing so deep my mouth falls open, my thighs squeezing and my heels scrambling for leverage beneath the blanket on the chaise.

But before I can respond, a light goes on farther down the boat.

And it's moving toward us.

My throat closes.

"Someone's coming." I grab Harrison's arm in warning.

"Yes. You."

The one thing crazier than letting Harrison King finger-fuck me on his rented yacht is having someone catch us.

The crew member pauses a dozen feet away. "Mr. King. Ms. Madani. Would you like anything to eat or drink before we retire?"

I shift, trying to straighten both of us, but my companion doesn't budge. Including the parts of him inside me. I feel every inch of his fingers as he holds me in place like a butterfly pinned to cloth.

"We're fine." Harrison's even reply suggests he does this all the time.

His front presses against my back. I can feel the impossibly thick outline of his erection, his heart thudding through our clothes and skin.

She smiles. "All right. Have a wonderful evening."

His mouth is at my ear the second she departs, his voice heated. "You think men like me rent forty-five-meter yachts to not fuck on them?"

I reach back with one hand to grab his hair. "*Charter.*"

His exhale is half laugh and half groan as his thumb drags a slow circle over my clit and he works my entrance with both fingers.

Oh my God.

I've seen Harrison playful before, and it's fascinating. But now, he's playing with *me*. My body is a game, and only he knows the rules. He's teaching them to me one skilled move at a time.

It feels way too damn good.

The orgasm sneaks up on me, a wave I'm thoroughly unprepared for. My toes squeeze under the blanket as I clench around him, my back arching. He growls his satisfaction against my cheek, his other hand cupping my breast, his thumb absently rubbing my nipple. I gasp as he draws out my pleasure almost painfully.

Each wave grips me in turn.

I'm so consumed with sensation I don't notice the computer slide off my lap.

"Motherfucker!" I jerk upright at the sickening sound of it hitting the deck. Horror slices through the bliss as I tumble off the lounger onto my knees to retrieve it before looking at him with accusing eyes. "This better not be broken." At least it's backed up.

Harrison's voice is languid. "I'll buy you a new one."

"You can't fix my problems with money, King."

"Watch me, Queen."

The expression on his handsome face makes my heart skip. Lust, satisfaction, and an emotion more than both. He's cocky, but beneath the surface is a genuine will to please me, a simple gratitude for this moment.

"That was... unexpected."

His slow grin is wicked in the dark. "Really? Because I've been picturing nothing else for weeks."

Harrison takes the computer from me and sets it gently on the end of the lounger. "Time for your real gift."

I turn to stare at him. "You're shitting me."

He rises and disappears belowdecks, returning a minute later with a box a little smaller than my computer, wrapped in velvet and a gold ribbon.

"Open it."

He draws me between his thighs again and tucks the blanket in around us as I tug at the ribbon until it gives way. The velvet wrapping is a bag, and I unfold it and slide out the box inside.

He waits patiently while I open it.

In the low lighting, the black Sennheiser logo is just visible against the impossibly shiny silver of the headphones, but it's the sparkling letters across the earpieces that grab my attention.

"I called the CEO and had him make them for you," Harrison says under his breath.

"Little Queen," I murmur, tracing the word on each side with a fingertip. Each letter is spelled out in a dozen tiny gems. "In crystals?"

"No."

Harrison's abs clench under me, and I lift my gaze to his, disbelieving.

"Tell me you didn't get me diamond headphones."

His eyes aren't cold tonight. They're warm like the sea, teeming with life and possibility.

"You're the real thing. Don't fucking forget it."

My chest aches.

I'm on a yacht celebrating with friends who flew halfway around the world to be with me, and it's all thanks to a billionaire I should hate. Except he's not the man he lets the public believe he is, and he just gave me the most incredible headphones and the most incredible orgasm.

But it's his words that affect me more than anything we've done.

"Did you make a wish on your birthday candle?" he prompts when I'm silent.

I hook the headphones around my neck

because I can't stand to put them down. "I haven't believed in that since I was a kid."

He pulls my back to his front, and I relax into him, lifting my chin to stare at the stars overhead.

"Then it's time to start again," he decides, tucking a piece of hair behind my ear.

Maybe he's right.

Before I fall asleep, I send up a wish.

19

HARRISON

"You were a difficult man to contact this weekend," Christian says from the end of the dinner table.

"I spent a few days on a yacht."

There are hints a man is mortal if you know where to look.

Tonight, the *sirvia* is overcooked.

When I bite into the fish, I know there's a crack in Christian Geroux's facade.

This weekend, I felt the cracks in myself with Rae. Spending time with her and her friends, I found myself caring less about my need to conquer and claim every property Mischa has so much as glanced at and more about her.

"I didn't realize you were a seaman." Mischa,

opposite me, digs into his fish as if it's still alive and he wishes it was.

Like me, he's in a suit, his a gray so dark it's nearly black. His pocket square is red. A signature. I heard a tailor once tried to influence his style. The man died of a heart attack the next week.

"He hates being on the water," my ex weighs in from next to Mischa.

It's the world's most fucked-up dinner. Mischa, my ex, Christian, his wife, and their youngest daughter Sylvie.

We're here to talk business, ostensibly to finalize plans for La Mer. But Christian's not ready to divest or divulge anything until after dinner and drinks.

"So, what made you do it?" Christian muses. "I thought Harrison King did only what he wished."

I reach for my *vino blanco*, but someone else answers first.

"A woman."

We turn toward Sylvie.

"It's the only reason other than business that a man does what he does not want to do," she goes on. "Even business is in service of his ultimate pleasure."

Perhaps she's not as naïve as I figured.

"Pursuing a woman is in service of a man's ultimate pleasure too." Mischa grins at my ex, who allows it, but she cuts a look at me the moment he drops her eyes.

I couldn't care less about them tonight. For the past two days, I've let myself live in an alternate world. Seasickness aside, it was enthralling. Spending time with Rae's group—most of them successful, all of them hardworking and earnest.

Rae was at the heart of it all.

Those dark eyes loaded with willfulness. Her soft curves making my hands burn to touch her.

That night on the deck, her jealousy over Sylvie was laughable.

It also made me hard as steel.

When Rae settled between my thighs, I couldn't help myself. My hands trailed down between her legs, needing to know if she felt the scorching intensity I did.

The damp heaven I found there was the sweetest fucking temptation. The way she let me touch her, then rubbed against me for more.

It's not only the promise of sex that captures me. It's the way she challenges me. I can show her things, but she's no wallflower. Every time I push her, she shoves back harder.

Most women want what I can give them—the trappings of my world.

Rae doesn't want them.

I can't buy her affection. Instead, I'm toiling for

every inch of trust she parcels out in a muttered admission or an allowed touch.

I don't know who hurt her in her life before she took my stage.

When I find out, I will bury them.

My parents were good people who provided everything for me and Ash. I'll never be a saint, but thanks to their influence, I look after my own. A small group that expanded to include Rae while I wasn't looking.

Her final show is coming up, and I'm not ready for it.

I don't want her to go.

"At the risk of sounding patriarchal," Christian says, his voice dragging me back, "the men will now talk business in the library."

Our plates are cleared, my ex murmuring her appreciation. "The sirvia was excellent."

Fucking liar.

Mischa and I follow Christian to the library, where we take seats.

Christian doesn't waste time with more small talk. "La Mer is the jewel in my collection. Forty years ago, I would have dreamed about having two businessmen such as yourselves vying for it. Alas, men become greedy, and I am but a man. So, with two such suitors, I must weigh the relative offers."

He shifts back in his leather chair. Despite the

words, he enjoys holding court.

"There are day-to-day concerns with a club of this size. For instance, millions in revenues. I have a request of you both first. Consider it a practical test."

I shift forward.

"We lost a performer due to unforeseen circumstances and must find someone suitable to put in his place. The long weekend."

"The big producers have been booked for months. Years." But my mind is already scanning through possibilities. Between Leni and me, we could probably call in a favor.

"I'll find the perfect act." Mischa's teeth are bared in my direction, but not in a grin. He'd like to hurt me right now, but we're not boys in school anymore. Even if he wanted to make this physical, he wouldn't dare. It's an unspoken rule that we fight our war with money and strategy, not with blades or blood.

Christian strokes his chin. "I would like to speak to each of you in turn about your vision for my venue. Mischa first. Harrison," he goes on before I can argue, "allow my daughter to refresh your drink while you wait."

I rise, fastening my jacket with one hand. Each stride toward the door is tight with frustration.

Sylvie greets me in the hallway with a tentative

smile. "I'll get you a drink from the kitchen."

I follow her there and help by retrieving the bottle she wants from a shelf. The moment I set it on the counter, her mouth is on mine.

She's innocent and determined, and I hold her arms gently as I push her away. "I can't."

Her expression caves. "You don't find me attractive."

"It's not that. There's someone else."

The light in her eyes dies.

I pour a drink and hand it to her. "Perhaps you could use this more than me."

She accepts it with a tiny nod.

I was going to pump her for information, but the sadness on her face makes me reconsider.

When did I go soft? I wonder as she heads toward the patio.

"Lovers' quarrel?" A familiar voice interrupts my thoughts. "What a shame. You'd be perfect together."

I turn to see my ex hovering in the hall.

Her blue cocktail dress compliments curves I once memorized. Now, Eva is a piece of art that doesn't resonate—the objective quality is irrefutable, yet she leaves me cold and unmoved.

"I'd run right over her."

"Precisely. You need a woman who lets you be the man you are."

"Like you did?" I'm surprised to hear there's no bitterness in my voice.

She frowns. "A woman who wants all of you will never have you. You are on this earth with a purpose, and you will die to fulfill it. You would never die for me."

I smirk. "Who would've bought you jewelry if I had?"

"A woman who demands more from you... you'd wear one another down."

I turn that over. "Perhaps that's the point. Sanding one another's roughest edges doesn't make you weaker—it makes you better."

The door of the study cracks down the hall, and I turn my back on Eva's stunned expression.

"Mr. King?" Christian beckons, and I trade places with a smug-looking Mischa.

I ignore the seat my host offers, instead resting an elbow on the back of the armchair. "I have a DJ for La Mer. She's young, but she's talented. Capable. Charismatic."

I tell him about Rae's success filling the club while he listens thoughtfully.

"You are quite taken with her."

"I'm confident she'll be an asset to the stage." I pause, unable to read him. "You want to hear my vision for the club? Here it is—"

"Marry Sylvie and the club is yours."

I'm stunned silent. Of the things I expected he'd ask in exchange for his club, this isn't one of them.

Christian continues. "Not immediately, of course. Court her. Take what time you need. What time you both need. I worked hard on my business and my family. This club is like another of my children. I want to see it in the right hands."

Sylvie's attempts at seduction in the kitchen were sweet, if wholly misguided. But the man before me is serious.

I don't point out the archaic nature of what he's proposing—his child for his club. Clearly whatever her father said to her made her think I would be an attractive partner. And she's not alone in that.

Women take a look at me and decide who and what I am, whether it's money, an attractive package, a ticket to the right social circles.

I never had a problem with it.

I spent months engaged to a woman more caustic than Sylvie could ever be, one with ambitions that clashed with mine, though she hid them well. Christian's daughter would be more loyal, and amenable.

But it's none of those thoughts that has my body clenching in denial.

It's the thought of another woman entirely.

One who sees what I am on the surface and insists I could be more.

One who wants me *in spite of* my money and power.

One I may never be with… but ruling that out entirely feels like a rip in my soul.

"I can't be with your daughter, Christian," I say at last. "She's lovely and intelligent, and she'll find someone well suited to her." *Without your help*, I don't add. "But that man isn't me."

He sighs. "That is indeed a disappointment. I was looking forward to the idea our empires might one day become one."

He's withdrawing. I feel it.

This can't be over. I won't lose La Mer this way.

Adrenaline pours through my veins.

"My parents were married in Ibiza," I hear myself say. "A small ceremony."

"I remember."

"After, they danced on the beach in the place La Mer now stands. When it opened, they thought it the ideal place—not a club, but an altar. A slice of heaven where the sea meets the sky."

Christian chuckles. "One you wish to possess."

"One Mischa doesn't deserve to." There's an edge of desperation to my voice. "He's playing to your vanity."

"And you to my morality? Surely there are

better men for that."

I circle the chair, shift onto the edge, and look the man dead in the eyes. "My father was your colleague. Your friend. You were business partners occasionally. Friends always."

His gaze sharpens. "Friendship is easy to portray. A smile here. A handshake there. I'm sure there are moments you and Mischa could be mistaken for friends, in a polite room."

The hairs on my neck rise. Was there bad blood between him and my father? If so, that's news to me.

I regroup, vowing to get to the bottom of that later.

"Think about my recommendation. I stand behind her unreservedly."

He rubs his chin, eyes altogether too knowing. "If you are certain she's available, I will consider it."

I nod. "I'll make sure of it."

Despite the unresolved nature of the La Mer deal, conviction surges through me.

Now, I have a reason to ask her to stay.

On my way out of the study, I nearly run into Mischa, who's waiting in the hallway.

I don't know how much he heard, but as I start down the hall, his dead eyes leave holes in my back.

20

———

RAE

"Impossible." Leni drops onto a stool at the VIP room bar, putting a shot of tequila in front of me.

"What is?"

"We broke sixteen hundred on Monday," she reminds me. "Tonight, we're at eighteen hundred and you haven't even taken the stage yet. There's a line around the hotel."

We clink glasses and toss them back.

"At least I can go out on a high note," I say after I swallow, the alcohol burning down my throat. "Thank you for this."

I'm a few minutes from my final performance at Debajo, and it's bittersweet.

In a month, this place has become familiar in a way I never asked for. The leather seats of the VIP stools creak predictably. I know the names of all the security guards and most of the bartenders. Even Leni and I have become more acquainted through working on concepts for my nights here.

"You know that having you close on a Saturday was Harrison's idea," Leni says. Under my stare, she finally rolls her eyes. "Fine, I didn't argue much. You're going to be big. It's clear to anyone who watches you. You're not so Little, Little Queen."

She nods to my outfit, a fitted, sleeveless gold dress with a raven black wig, plus eyeliner that makes my eyes look even darker than usual. It's a subtle channeling of another queen.

"It wasn't a snake bite," Leni says. "Cleopatra, I mean. The artists tell whatever stories they want," she waves a hand in the air, "but she poisoned herself. A tragic end."

"A realistic one," I correct. "The most powerful people spend their lives fighting external battles. It's the internal ones that get them."

Leni clunks the empty glass back on the bar. "You should stick around for the rest of the summer. We could find a couple nights a week for you here."

Surprise sets me back. "I have some other gigs lined up in July and August, but nothing for a few weeks. I guess I'd have to talk with Harrison. I haven't seen much of him in the last couple of days."

He said he's been working on persuading Christian to sell him La Mer.

"Since your birthday." She rises with a wink, nodding toward the headphones around my neck.

I've barely taken them off because they're precious in a way that has nothing to do with the diamonds I can't begin to value.

But as she goes, I stare after her, wondering exactly how much Harrison told her.

I know he and Leni go back, that she's the right hand of his business, but what happened on that yacht is personal. At least it was for me.

The birthday party was spectacular, but the part that left the biggest impression was the time I spent with him on the top deck that night.

I'm supposed to leave in two more days, and maybe that's the last moment we're meant to have together.

If it was, I should be grateful. When I arrived here and learned who I'd be playing for, I thought there was no way I'd make it through the month.

Now, I've turned around this club that deserves to be full, earned enough money to help my cousin keep the doors of her charity open, and met a man who makes me question everything.

That's why I don't want to think my birthday

was our last night together. I'm not ready to let him go.

I shove it from my mind and put the finishing touches on my set.

When I get to the stage, I'm home. The crowd erupts, delight on the faces of hundreds of men and women.

The music is in me, around me, consuming me.

The countless hours I put in were worth it.

Tonight, in this club that's as close to mine as anything ever was, pieces of that persona fall away.

I love this club.

The patrons love me.

It's not enough.

When I look up toward the VIP section, Harrison's leaning over the railing.

My heart kicks in my chest at the fact that he's here.

I wanted to believe he wouldn't miss this but couldn't be sure.

He's alone tonight, dressed in another impeccable suit. The bespoke armor clings to every inch of his hard body. Those shadowed eyes bore into mine as if he knows me.

I want to be known.

"Eighteen hundred!" I holler, my voice lost in

the pulsing beat and driving bass and throbbing melody of the club.

There's no way he can hear me, but he lifts a glass in my direction.

I never thought it would feel so damn good to have this moment and, more than that, to share it with someone.

When I flip both middle fingers in the air, his smirk fades.

He's too far away to read what's in his eyes, but he holds my gaze.

What passes between us is more than reciprocity. Connection, understanding, a tacit agreement that we built this together.

I want to celebrate with him. To tell him how fucking good it feels.

"You think you can teach me about sex?"

"No. I think I can teach you about yourself."

Each song bleeds into the next, and I bleed with them. When the set wraps, I don't know if it's been an hour or a year.

I'm energized and exhausted, sweaty and exhilarated.

I need to take selfies with fans, but as I trip out of the booth, someone beats me there.

The man looms over me in a designer suit, a shock of red silk in his breast pocket resembling a wound. "You are a rare talent."

He's all muscle, his head buzzed, his eyes cold. As if there's nothing behind them but emptiness.

I look over his shoulder at my waiting fans that security is holding at bay.

"I'm a friend of the owner," he says, answering my unasked question of how he got back here.

"Which friend?" I don't want to cause a scene, but I also don't want this prick in my face.

"I'm sure you don't know all Harrison King's friends."

"Try me."

His grip tightens on my wrist, and I twist away. He grabs my other wrist too, and I bite down on a cry of pain.

"I've been asking myself a question all day. Why would he give this up for you?"

He must be talking about Harrison, but I have no idea what he means.

My breathing is off the rhythm of the after-party song, but all I feel is my ribs expanding and contracting against the gold dress I chose at a boutique yesterday with Ash's help.

He pins me in the curtains backstage, his cloying cologne drowning me.

Sweat rolls down my neck, my body already straining to run. I reach for the only weapon I have —the defiance I've clung to for weeks, months.

"If you have a thing for Harrison," I manage, "you're out of luck. I don't think you're his type."

Fireworks explode behind my eye socket, impossible heat blossoming across my cheek. The physical impact stuns me.

On the other side of the stage, security is dealing with the crowd and giving me a minute to get ready.

I wish they weren't.

"You think I don't know what to do with bitches?" my attacker spits.

This isn't happening.

Do something.

No one answers my silent plea.

The man hulks closer, his body looming large and threatening.

Do something!

This time, I'm screaming at myself.

When he comes at me, I dig my fingernails into his neck. He bellows, his hand flying to the wounds.

They're not deep enough to keep him occupied long, and he's about to land another blow when there's motion at the curtains.

The next second, my attacker is gone.

Harrison drags the man out of the curtains, tossing him against the front row of the crowd. The patrons stare as the owner of the club pulls back a fist and looses it on the man before him.

The man lurches, listing as if he's been drinking before straightening with a cruel grin. "Is that it?"

It's his opponent's turn to land a punch, leaving a streak of blood across Harrison's cheek. My heart hammers until I realize it's the other man's. From where he was covering his neck.

Harrison barely stumbles before straightening. Even without the tic in his jaw, the heavy breathing, the icy fire in Harrison's eyes would be terrifying.

He grabs the other man by the collar, dragging him close to whisper something I can't make out. Then Harrison hits him again, hard enough the man topples.

Harrison shakes out his hand, his grim expression cast in the semidarkness of the club.

"Get him the fuck out of here, or you'll never work again," he bites out to security.

Across the crowd, Leni runs interference, trying to get things back to normal despite the fight that broke out.

My back hits a speaker, and I shift up onto it, my hands curling into my stomach. The sight of blood under my fingernails makes my stomach lurch.

I didn't feel the full effects of fear when everything was happening so fast, but now I do.

I haven't felt that fear in a decade, but it's fresh. A forgotten record pulled out of a box and set beneath a needle to play as fully and crisply as the day it was inscribed.

There's a bucket of waters in ice next to the speaker, and I force myself to reach for one as my cheek throbs.

Before I can press it to my face, the curtains move.

My head snaps up.

Harrison's usual elegance is rumpled. His shirt has lost two buttons, his jacket hanging haphazardly from his shoulders as if it refuses to let go. His hair is sticking up as he rubs a hand across his jaw, each knuckle dark with blood.

He closes the distance between us, stopping when my shins brush the tailored fabric of his dress pants. He inspects my face, lingering on my cheekbone that feels as if it might explode.

He's a king tonight, and for the first time, I see its weight on his face, his bones.

"You're hurt." The words are forceful, but strained. His eyes narrow on the unopened water bottle in my hands. "Where did he touch you?"

When I don't answer, his hands go to work searching for damage.

I stiffen as his touch roams my bare arms first, then my torso, finding a rip in my dress I hadn't noticed.

He shrugs out of his jacket and loops it around my shoulders, warming me before I realize I was shivering.

Then he presses between my thighs, lifts my skirt.

My mouth falls open as he runs his hands up my thighs. It's confident, competent, not meant to arouse but to assess.

"Stop," I whisper.

The backs of my eyes burn. Outside, I'm as frozen as the moment the man came at me. Not in fear, but in shock.

"Harrison, don't touch me." I want to scream the words but when they come out, they're barely audible.

It takes everything in me to grab his face and force his attention up even as his hands linger under my skirt.

His jaw clenches as he leans his forehead against mine. "I need to know you're all right."

I'm not.

I don't say it, but I might as well have.

The shaking starts somewhere in my chest and radiating out to reach my fingers, my toes, my lips.

Without warning, his arms are around me.

He lifts me, carrying me through the crowd before I can protest.

Leni grabs him on our way past. "Harrison, the police need to talk to you!"

"Tomorrow."

Then we're through the door and outside.

He settles me into the Ferrari, and I yank at the pins securing my wig with shaking hands.

Then I throw all of it on the floor and stare at the pile the entire way back.

"I can walk," I murmur when Harrison opens my car door at the villa.

He loops an arm around my waist, unwilling to let me support myself.

We step inside and Barney trots sleepily to the door, whining when neither of us reaches down to pet him.

Harrison helps me out of my shoes and up the stairs, but when I try to turn toward my room, he pulls me gently the other way.

"I have first aid equipment in my bathroom."

Of the ways I imagined seeing his space for the first time, this never entered my mind.

There's dark wood furniture, a dresser and

night tables without photos or adornment. A tufted area rug that's soft beneath my bare feet.

My brainpower is limited, a highway reduced from four lanes to two for some unauthorized repair.

Harrison seats me on an enormous bed with navy covers. "Don't move."

He disappears, returning a moment later with ice from the kitchen. I shift over to let him on the bed, but instead he kneels on the floor, lifting the ice to my cheek.

The cold burns my bruised flesh.

I take the ice from him, and he gently slides the jacket off my shoulders, then reaches around me for the zipper on my dress. I suck in a breath but don't argue as he drags it down.

Tonight was supposed to be my crowning achievement. A victory lap.

Now, it's tainted.

He shifts my hips so he can lift the hem, work it up my body and over my head.

Another inspection begins, more thorough than the one he did at the club.

"So that was Mischa," I guess, mostly to make sure I can still speak.

Harrison's attention lingers on my side as he nods. I didn't think I could take his touch, but being here, safe in his home, every stroke of his hands helps to steady my breathing.

"No offense, but I hope he's not the only friend you kept from school."

Harrison huffs out a breath at my attempt at humor.

He takes my hand with the ice and lowers it, brushing his thumb over my half-stinging, half-numb cheek. "Did he speak to you?"

A memory scratches at my brain. "He said you gave something up for me. What did he mean?"

Harrison doesn't answer. But when he lifts his clear, blue gaze, the anger's gone. "I never should have brought you here, Raegan."

He's inches away, but it feels like he's putting more distance between us with every breath.

The sudden ache in my chest eclipses the pain in my face.

Moments ago, I wanted to erase tonight. But he wants to erase the past month.

All of my time in Ibiza, my time with him.

His jacket in the pool. Our kiss at La Mer. My birthday on the yacht.

The tragedy of that hits me harder than anything else.

I don't want to forget.

That thought has me straightening, lends me the strength I've been seeking for the last hour.

"You're an asshole," I decide. The words land between us, raw and loaded. "You think you decide everything? That you have all the answers? You don't get to decide what this month meant. You don't sure as hell don't get to take this away from me."

I shove myself off the bed, ice burning my hand, and head for the door.

He beats me there, filling the doorway. "Take what away?"

I don't want to talk, and I can't stand the distance he's putting between us as he tries to reason out what happened tonight.

There's no reason to be found in violence.

I grab his neck and drag him down to me.

He stiffens when our lips collide, surprise evident in every inch of his taut body.

His breath mingles with mine. He's fighting his need, every bit as determinedly as he fought the man at the club.

Whatever we've become in these short weeks is real.

The moment of danger, of remembering that all I am could be gone in a moment...

I won't lose it without experiencing this.

I rub my shuddering body against his.

The words I can't say are clutched in my grasping hands, clinging to my desperate lips.

I've never begged Harrison for anything, but now, I am. I'm demanding and pleading in the same breath.

"Fuck, Raegan."

The moment he takes control, my heart skips in warning, in anticipation.

His tongue thrusts inside my mouth. His groan reverberates through my body, his need colliding with mine.

I want him in me everywhere with the same driving possession.

I grab his hair to change the angle between us, seeking relief even as he chases more friction.

When his hands slide up my legs, no longer inspecting but *memorizing*, the hunger inside me grows into something alive and throbbing.

The ice falls from my fingers to the floor. My hands run down his untucked shirt before sneaking beneath to caress the hard lines of his abs. Harrison groans, pressing his hips closer.

"So many buttons," I mutter as I work off his shirt.

He shoves my hands away and rips the garment down the front.

This isn't sweet—it's a race to the bottom. The only relief we'll find tonight is the kind we can give each other.

He backs me into the wall, his hands racing over my breasts, my pebbled nipples.

His fingers settle between my thighs, rubbing through the wet panel of lace.

My face hurts, my body shivers, but his capable fingers make me ache—for more, for him.

He drags my panties down, the lace digging into my hips.

"Fucking beautiful," he murmurs once they're gone.

Appreciation isn't what I need from him.

He's a storm I can't control—but he's one I can choose.

I reach for his belt, fumbling until it falls loose. I drag the zipper down over his straining length.

When my hand closes around him, my throat dries.

He's strong and male and undeniable. The arousal beading at his tip is for me. The tension in every inch of his glorious body and the fierce possession in his eyes is mine alone.

For the first time outside of a DJ booth, I feel powerful.

Harrison reaches for the bedside table on a hiss, returning to rip at a package and toss the wrapper to the floor.

He rolls the condom down his length, then lifts

me against the wall, encouraging me to hook my legs around him.

My head hits the edge of a picture frame. Harrison bats at the frame until it slides down the wall and hits the floor with a thud.

He grabs my hip, positioning himself between my thighs. "Need you now."

It's a warning or a declaration, because the next second, he thrusts.

He's big and thick. My body has to stretch to take him the way he's demanding.

Every inch he buries inside me is one more reminder he's unlike any man I've experienced.

My back arches, my nails digging into his arms hard enough to leave marks.

"God, you're slick." His voice is thick with arousal.

Pleasure and pain blur, the throbbing core of need deep inside me the only thing I feel.

He withdraws, a slow drag, then shifts back in on a groan.

His jaw works, and I don't know if it's from the effort of what we're doing or the effort of holding back.

It's decadent and brutal, his muscled body pinning mine. Giving and taking. Daring and fulfilling.

He bends his head to bite the curve of my breast, and my body clenches around him.

My legs ache.

Wallpaper scratches my back.

Sweat has my fingers slipping on his.

The more I writhe, the tighter he holds me. His lips skim my neck, my jaw, my ear.

I was already close to shattering tonight, and I thought this was what I needed.

But it's not. It's more.

He's over me, inside me, around me, part of me. This man I thought was the last person I'd ever trust.

Every punishing stroke of his hips chases away my fear, his regret.

It's another few strokes before I arch, my climax starting at my core and rippling outward.

He moves through it, hips thrusting faster, deeper. I shudder with every movement of his gorgeous body.

The pace is relentless until the moment he freezes over me, going still. His jaw clenches in anguish as his release rips through him.

I'm in awe. It's as if I'm seeing him for the first time.

When he shifts forward, his lips brushing my ear as he groans, "Fuck, Raegan," I wrap my limbs around him to hold him there.

After, he pulls down the covers and tucks me into bed before heading for the bathroom. I hear the sound of the sink, water running, then nothing.

I stare at the ceiling, my heart echoing in the darkness.

I feel...alive.

Instead of healing me, what we did made a new edge, bright and gleaming and raw.

The difference is this edge is exhilarating. Full of possibility.

But most of all...

I'm not alone.

It feels like an epiphany.

When he returns, reaching for his discarded clothes, the feeling deflates.

"You're leaving?" I ask quietly.

"I have to talk to the police. Leni texted to say it can't wait until morning." He dresses quickly and competently, knotting his tie and adjusting it. Every motion is as smooth and natural as how he moved inside me moments ago. "I'll be back before you wake."

The wave of anxiety sneaks up on me, settles into a vicious knot in my chest. I press a fist to my ribs under the sheets and silently count each shallow breath. "Promise?"

His gaze flicks to mine.

I'm not the woman who needs anyone's assurance. But now, in the dark, after what happened tonight... I'm not ready to be alone.

Whatever he sees on my face has him crossing to me, pressing a soft kiss to my lips.

"I promise."

Then he's gone.

21

RAE

I've had a lot of sleepless nights. I was prepared for this to be among the worst.

But when I roll from my back onto my side, the first thing I notice is warm, golden light.

The soreness creeping into my awareness is the second. The spot between my thighs aches, but so does my face.

I blink my eyes open to see pale curtains waving in the breeze from the half-opened window, beckoning me into the world.

The scent of Harrison King lingering on the pillows makes me want to press my face into the covers.

But he's not here.

I sit up. There's no clock, but judging by the

light, it's late. I reach for my phone on the bedside table to see if he's texted.

He hasn't.

But there's another slate of messages.

Callie: WTF is going on?

Followed by a link.

Confusion crowds into the worry as I click the link she sent, waiting for the article to load.

Feminist DJ Caught with Businessman She Trolled: Was It All a PR Stunt?

It's by the reporter I met in person here in Ibiza. I barely have time to process that before the photos load.

The first is of me in the booth at the club last night. It's my wig, along with my gold dress, and I look powerful. It's the kind of shot clubs want for their promotions, that makes people groan they missed out on the hottest party and line up for next week's tickets.

The second photo is darker and harder to make out.

A woman, seated on something dark and out of frame, her dress high enough to expose her legs. Legs wrapped around a man in an untucked dress shirt, his dirty-blond hair and sharp bone structure visible in profile.

His hand is fisted in her hair, the other on her hip beneath the edge of the gold dress, just visible beneath the jacket wrapped around her shoulders.

They could be fucking. He could be deep inside her the moment this image was taken, his grip on her helping him chase his release.

Except they're not, because they're us. Harrison and me in a moment I never imagined being captured by another person. But the photo was taken last night at the club.

As I read the article, my breath comes so shallowly I might as well not be breathing at all.

The text cites an incident at his LA club this week. Plus, a list of issues at his other properties.

My lips tremble.

He said it was getting better.

And I trusted him.

Every line of the article guts me more than the last. It doesn't outright call me a slut—which would've pissed me off but not hurt. Instead, I'm a hypocrite. I called out the man running the show only to cave to him, let him control me, at the first opportunity.

That's not what this was.

Unable to stomach any more, my face throbbing in earnest now, I click out of the story.

The final text message rips my heart in half.

Callie: Tell me you're not with that man. Did he hurt you? Pressure you?

I shut off the phone and head to the closet and grab one of Harrison's dress shirts, slipping it on.

I slowly turn the door handle and step silently into the hallway.

There are noises downstairs, and suck in a breath. "Harrison?"

Natalia appears at the doorway of the kitchen, looking worried. "Señorita. Toro went to take him from the police station hours ago."

"Take him where?"

She dries her hands on a towel. "I don't know."

"But he's all right?"

"I believe so."

He's fine.

The knot in my chest eases, only to retighten.

He's fine, and he didn't return.

I head for my room, where I stare at the article again.

My throat aches. The stinging spots on my cheeks are tears.

I reach for the untouched bottle of pills on my dresser, fumbling with the lid. I take one dry.

The article wasn't entirely correct… but it wasn't all wrong either. Last night might not have been a PR stunt, but I did get caught up in something I was too naïve to handle.

I believed what I wanted to believe. I trusted a man I had no business trusting. Got comfortable in a place I never should have stayed.

I call him again.

He picks up on the third ring.

"Hello—"

"Harrison, I need you." I choke out the words, but his voice continues.

It's voicemail.

"You've reached Harrison King. I recommend you don't leave a message. If I need you, I will find you."

If I need you, I will find you.

He clearly doesn't, because he's not here.

22

———

HARRISON

By the time I'm finished with the police, I want nothing more than my home and the woman waiting for me there.

Rae and I have things to discuss, things we didn't get to last night.

Still, I have to make one stop on the way. There's something I haven't been able to shake, something made more real by Mischa's appearance last night—an act not of calculation but of desperation.

"If you're following up about your suggestion of a DJ, I've considered it. She's not ready."

Christian's voice comes from the doorway of his study.

I snap shut the book I was pretending to read.

"She is. She filled Debajo for the first time in years."

"Debajo is not La Mer."

"No. It's harder. It was empty. Desolate." And it came with me. "Give her the chance. I promise she won't disappoint you."

"You would risk your reputation in this?"

"Yes."

"Then have her meet me this afternoon. We can discuss it."

Grim satisfaction grips me. I have no doubt Rae will convince him.

"I'm surprised you're not with her now."

Seeing Mischa looming over her at Debajo set a cold fury loose in me I haven't felt since my parents died.

I wanted to kill him.

But I wanted to save her more.

The irony didn't escape me, because it was my fault she was hurt. Mischa heard me admit to Christian that... what? I care for her?

He overestimated what I meant and went after her.

Or he didn't overestimate it.

All I knew was I needed to get her home, to make sure she was safe and comfortable.

But when I took her upstairs, the girl from the club slowly melted away, replaced with the woman

I've come to admire and appreciate and fucking hunger for.

I had no right to ask her for anything, but her raw response ripped away what was left of my control.

"I'll be with her soon," I promise Christian, picturing her asleep in my bed now.

I'll make it up to her—last night, and everything else I've done.

Including how I claimed her against the wall in a furious, graceless rush.

There are countless ways I've imagined being with her, a thousand temptations to explore together that would take more than a single night, not to mention a single hour, to enjoy.

Her term at Debajo is concluded. On paper, we might be finished.

In reality...

We're far from it. And now I have a reason to keep her here while we figure that out.

I start for the door, but Christian's voice interrupts me. "Is that what you came to say?"

I pause. "If things escalate with Mischa," I say, "know that I wasn't the one who initiated. Since school, we've kept things civilized. But I want La Mer. And if he won't play by the rules, I can't promise to."

"Breaking the rules. You come by it honestly."

I frown, ripples of discontent making me turn back. "Tell me what you meant about my father yesterday."

The older man crosses to the windows, peering out into the bright morning. "He's not the paragon of virtue you seem to think."

"My parents were above reproach. The second they learned about the drugs and other activities the Ivanov family was running behind the scenes, they wanted out. They would've died rather than supporting that kind of evil."

In the end, they did.

But Christian's silence is unsettling.

"You idolized them," he says at last. "It's dangerous to paint anyone as more than human. Particularly those we love."

I don't have the time to argue with him now, or to play games.

"If I promise to prove you wrong about my parents, promise me you won't sell the club to anyone else in the interim," I say. "You're a patient man. Give me the benefit of the same."

This deal is everything. I will him to agree.

"You have three months," he says, sighing.

I stride out of his house and out to the waiting limo.

The ride back feels interminable. I glance at my phone, seeing the barrage of missed calls as a result of turning alerts off for the morning to deal with more important things than business.

They don't matter.

I picture Rae's face when I tell her about Christian's offer to meet. This could be the single most important show of her career. It won't make up for last night, but it's a start.

The second we pull up to my villa, Natalia is out front, wringing her hands.

"Señor King." She crosses to the car, her expression a mask of distress.

"What is it?" I think the worst. Rae. She's hurt, or sick, or...

I shove past her and stomp inside, looking all around.

Nothing is out of the ordinary.

There's not a single item of Rae's clothing on a table or chair.

My chest twinges. A warning.

I take the stairs two at a time to my room. The bed is empty, the sheets rumpled.

I pace down the hall to the room at the other end, bypassing every other door as if they don't exist.

Hers is ajar, and that small crack of light fills me with trepidation.

I open the door, and my heart stops. There're

no messes, no clothes. No computer. No bottle of pills.

The closet is empty, save the dress and shoes I bought her to attend Christian's party.

Impossible.

The woman I slept with last night. The one I sacrificed for, the one I denied the man who owns the club I want more than anything else in the world for...

She's fucking gone.

Thank you for reading *Beautiful Enemy*! I hope you loved Harrison and Rae's love story as much as I do.

NEXT UP FOR HARRISON AND RAE...

CHAPTER ONE
Rae

The cable is loose. It's fucking irritating. What kind of club doesn't have the right gear?

The kind I used to play when I was hustling to get where I am.

Where I was until last month.

This is the best of the three gigs I've played since returning to LA. The caliber of clubs I've booked has gone down since the article released featuring the photo of Harrison and me backstage at Debajo.

My renewed infamy has created a new roadblock. Now I'm not just the woman who might publicly call out a club on their bullshit.

I'm also a hypocrite.

Still, we're in LA, and this venue is full of beautiful people in various stages of intoxication.

A small film crew occupies one side. Beck's in the center, security watching him and the crew surrounding him.

The entire set, the loose cable bugs me. Every minute, I expect the music to cut out and a bunch of partiers to throw their designer vodka drinks in my face.

But hey, at least I get to do what I love.

A month after what happened with Mischa, I

still get tense during the changeover, doing a scan of the crowd before I unplug and give up the stage to descend into the throng of partiers.

Tonight, there's a college-aged kid who leans too close, trying to look down the loose black shirt that's sticking to me with sweat.

A duo of guys flanks me, making God knows what symbol over my head while they snap a pic.

A young, platinum-blond woman drags her friends over. They shift from one deadly high heel to the other while she squeals.

"Girl, I'm a huge fan! Will you be at Wild Fest next year?"

I fix on a "we're all having fun here" smile I learned from Beck. "You'll have to wait and see."

"Ohmigod. It's going to be the biggest thing." She makes a duck face next to me as she wraps an arm around my shoulders. "I want life lessons from anyone who can land Harrison King. He's loaded and gorgeous and that accent... I bet he fucks like an animal."

As the flash goes off, I'm not seeing the camera or the woman.

All I can remember are the memories I've tried to shove down. Harrison King, body straining and damp with sweat, me clinging to him and gasping as he drove into me until we both collapsed.

But it was all a lie. It meant nothing.

"Dammit, one more?" the girl asks, but I'm already pushing away.

"Hey!" A whistle cuts through the noise, and I wait for Beck to catch up. "Heading out early?"

My friend is Hollywood-leading-man handsome, with dark hair and darker eyes that see more than they let on. His looks might've helped land him his primetime show, but his shrewdness got him the reality series he's filming now.

"Yeah. Thanks for bringing the crew here," I say.

The club made a few extra bucks, plus free publicity, for allowing Beck's crew to film an episode of the reality show here. If they didn't already want me back on the strength of my set, they will now.

"How many selfies did you take before someone brought your boy up?"

I shake my head. "It's been a month. He's living his life. I'm living mine." I eye his crew. "You should get back to the girl you were sucking face with. She's already bailed on her friends."

He glances back that way, where a beautiful, fresh-faced woman stands next to his security.

He goes to speak with her, then two minutes later, he's back, ushering me into the rear seat of a limo.

"Shouldn't have done that," I tell him as I drop

my bag on the floor and he reaches for a bottle of champagne in the fridge.

"You're my friend." He pops the cork and pours a glass, passing it to me. "So, I heard that chick ask about Wild Fest. *Are* you mixing there?"

I stare into the champagne flute, its tiny bubbles at odds with the leaden feeling inside me. "I got on their radar this spring before everything, but they've been dodging me since Ibiza."

"That's why you're pissy? It has nothing to do with Harrison King?"

"Nothing." I take a long drink, the bubbles tickling my throat, then burning after I swallow.

I pull off the headphones still around my neck and tuck them carefully into the bag at my feet.

Beck leans over, his handsome face suddenly close.

I frown. "What are you doing?"

"Testing your claim."

He covers my mouth with his.

His lips are determined and playful at once as he kisses me.

My hands freeze in midair, too stunned to do anything else. He dares me to pull back.

I let the feeling wash over me. He's warm, masculine, compelling in a totally unselfconscious, totally Beck way.

But it's not dangerous or breathtaking. My heart rate is up from surprise, not arousal.

When his tongue parts my lips, I shove at his chest.

Beck drops back against the seat with a laugh. "See? You're still hung up on the guy."

"Just because I don't want to fuck you doesn't mean I'm hung up on someone else."

"You're kidding, right? Have you seen me?"

His words eat at the wall around my heart. "Thanks for trying to make me feel better. Even if it was a fucked-up way to do it."

"I can't fix your heart, but I can say you have no reason to feel ashamed of what you did in Ibiza. Whatever makes you so critical started a long time ago with shit you don't think about in the light of the day, not to mention talk about."

"You get all that from me not letting you stick your tongue in my mouth?"

He shakes his head. "Been watching you a while, Little Queen. You haven't made peace with who you are. You want to play the Wild Fests of this world, you gotta do that sooner or later." His phone rings, and he mouths, "My producer," as he answers.

I drag out my own phone and pull up my social accounts.

Harrison King watch has resumed. He has left

Ibiza. Since the photos of us surfaced, he's been seen in London. Paris. At his clubs, but also with women.

What surprises me most is how the pictures make my chest ache. An unrelenting ache that lingers through days of trying to work, dinners with friends, nights alone.

How I feel has nothing to do with his hard, beautiful body or strong hands or firm lips or piercing blue eyes, and everything to do with the fact that I felt as if he showed me parts of himself he'd never shown anyone else.

Admitting what happened to his parents, that he's on a mission to redeem them. He'd do anything to win La Mer and rebuild the empire that fell when they died, the same empire I threatened when I exposed him on social media.

Anything—including using me.

I don't believe he set up the pictures of us at Debajo, but he must have seen them, and he hasn't reached out once.

Not a damn word. No defending what happened in his clubs or how it looked as if he used me.

I need to move on.

I haven't been up to New York because I know Annie will want to talk—the kind of talk with way too many feelings—and I'm avoiding getting into that.

Which is why I'm in a limo with Beck, who has not only given me a place to stay the past few weeks when I didn't want to be alone, but who should be fucking a perfectly nice girl instead of looking after me.

There's an email with a subject and sender that leap off the page.

"What's wrong?" Beck asks, and I realize he's hung up his call.

"My brother Kian's getting married in a month. He's inviting me."

"Short notice. Where's the wedding?"

"Napa." I fold my arms at his raised brow. "I grew up in Orange County."

His low rumble of laughter has me sighing. "You've been back a month, and I bet you haven't told any of them."

Shadows flick across his face from the streetlights, but it's the darkness inside me that makes me shiver.

"We haven't been close since high school."

Beck pulls my head down on his shoulder and lays his on top of mine. "Here's the thing. You could be a superstar. Have the Wild Fests of the world begging you to show. But you won't get there until you make peace with where you've been. No matter where you're going, you can't run from you."

"Have you made peace?" I ask him pointedly.

He's had trouble with his parents—they're flush and part of New York society, and from what I understand, having their son turn his back on the career his father wanted for him to pursue acting and come out publicly as bi pushed their self-righteous buttons.

He sighs. "Work in progress."

I grab the champagne and chug the rest, then turn off my phone and shove it in my bag, leaving the top open. The glint of diamond headphones follows me home.

CHAPTER TWO
Harrison

It's not the first time I've tried to open a new door in my life—metaphorically or literally.

Nor is it the first time the way has been thoroughly barricaded.

"How long will this take?" I bark into my Bluetooth headphones, kicking at the stack of cinderblocks barring the entrance to the warehouse.

"Depends. The documents you shared about

your parents weren't much to go on." The other man's Northern Irish accent abrades my ears.

"So go to other sources. You're the investigator." Cobwebs cover my hands as I lift a brick and set it a dozen feet away.

"You can't just go around asking whether dead people were involved in illicit activities."

I toss my tie over my shoulder as I bend to grab two more. "Should be easier than when they were alive."

My top priority is convincing Christian my parents were innocent so he'll sell me La Mer. Hence the investigator.

My father helped build the legitimate side of Mischa's family's business, acquiring and managing real estate and venues. I didn't think much of it until the summer after my fist year of uni in Connecticut. I arrived home to find them looking so drained even a self-indulgent nineteen-year-old would notice something was wrong.

They looked over their shoulders when we were out. Stayed in the living room, speaking in hushed tones late at night. While I had been at school, they'd become unhappy ghosts of the people who raised me.

Which was why I told them to leave the Ivanov family's business.

They were in the process of doing that when

they were killed, their deaths made to look like drug overdoses.

"Someone is alleging my parents not only knew the full nature of what transpired in that business but enabled it."

If anyone but Christian needed the kind of proof I hired the investigator to find, I'd have dismissed it as ugly conjecture. However, what Christian thinks matters because I need to buy his club in order to bury Mischa once and for all.

"You have thirty days to definitively return evidence they were innocent."

I click off more forcefully than necessary and toss the earpieces in my pocket as footsteps approach me from behind.

"Sounds juicy, boss." Leni pops a hand on a hip as I grab the last of the blocks blocking the door.

"Christian's holding out on La Mer. I thought he and my father were good friends. Turns out there was something between them. A misunderstanding, no doubt. My father was a decent man."

"And if he wasn't?"

I frown at the sun over the top of the warehouse, sweat making my shirt stick to my back. "Everything I'm doing to rebuild what they started is for them. I can't believe he would have knowingly helped build an empire on people's suffering." I grab my pocket square and wipe the dirt off my hands, the sweat at the base of my neck. "Digging up the truth is my investigator's business. In the meantime, this is ours."

She turns to survey the property. "Looks like shit."

"Most diamonds do before they're polished." I unlock the door and gesture inside. "After you."

The space is massive, a single open rectangle with concrete floors and industrial lighting suspended thirty feet up.

The floor plans I reviewed say there are offices at one end, which we can use. The dozen loading docks are overkill. We might use one, but the rest need to be closed off or redesigned.

"How long to renovate it into a nightclub?" I ask.

"Assuming the permits and zoning are lined up... a year."

"They're not, and I want it in six months."

Her laughter dies. "You're serious?"

"I'm not waiting around while Christian passes judgment. Echo will continue to expand. We've been making acquisitions, but we can't ignore development opportunities. This will be our next nightclub."

Rumors of the nightclub industry's downfall are overblown. The clubs that are closing are ones where the owners don't understand the business they're in and don't evolve to deliver their function in new ways.

A club isn't a venue that serves drinks.

It's a theme park.

A secret rendezvous.

Hell, even a runway.

It's a vehicle for thrills. The thrill made by being swept up in the darkness, the music, of watching and putting on a show.

Leni sighs. "I'll see what I can do about the timeline. Work our contractor contacts, assuming we can pay twice regular rates."

"One and a half," I correct. "I'll take care of the zoning and permits."

LA is a city built for that twisted intersection of the elegant and the hedonistic, the cultured and the primal.

This area includes some studio buildings and storage. It's close enough to Hollywood and most LA neighborhoods to get people in, and transit is established, though I expect most people will arrive by car.

Still, I've heard it's tough to get through the zoning committees. We need to show them that putting a mixed-use entertainment venue here will be an asset to the local community rather than a liability.

"Why are you even here, converting some

warehouse instead of running La Mer?" Leni prods. "I thought you and Christian were working it out."

"I told him I'd prove to him I could run it and suggested an artist who could step in for the long weekend."

"And?"

"And the day after I promised that, she left."

My feet echo on the concrete as I cross the space, heading for the doors at the far side.

Leni cocks her head. "Let me guess—she doesn't know about La Mer. Because your pride stopped you from telling her or from asking her to stay."

"It's not pride. She made it clear she wants nothing more to do with me."

I grimace as I reach the door labeled OFFICE, try the handle. It gives. I peer into the darkness, feeling for a light switch. When I find it, the over-head light clicks on, showing a surprisingly decent space with furniture still in place.

This summer with Raegan was unexpected. I might've been the one to trick her into playing Debajo, but the joke was on me.

I felt way too fucking much around her. Not only was she beautiful and talented and stubborn. I wanted to fix the damned world for her, to make myself and everything around me worthy.

None of it mattered because she left at the first opportunity.

It's unreasonable to blame her after what happened with Mischa. But I do.

I blame her.

Because whatever I felt, she didn't feel the same, or she would've stayed.

Leni passes me and drags a finger across the dusty desk. "Rae's playing in LA, you know."

My abs clench at the sound of her name.

When Rae left, I needed to get my head out of my ass and move on with my business. Part of that was being seen at events, which I squared my shoulders for and undertook. I needed to play the game and be seen playing it.

Still... Every suggestive look, every overt invitation from women in my social circle, I've turned down.

It's a strange combination, being available and being utterly uninterested in anyone but the one person I can't have.

"You've been a bear since she left. What're you going to do about it?"

I glare. "I liked you better when you weren't up in my business."

"You're the one who hired me. Still can't quite figure out why you picked up a bunch of misfits.

Me, Natalia, Toro, half the people in your business."

"My father always said to put the right people around you. I need a team that doesn't require coddling to do what has to be done."

Leni cocks a brow. "And she fits right in. Rae's tougher than I thought. I like her. And you do too, or you wouldn't have taken a sudden interest in a Burbank warehouse that's sat vacant since you bought it a year ago."

"I'm not here for her. This is business." I survey the room, imagining the dusty furniture replaced with more modern trappings.

"Let's pretend that's true. Rae's taken a hit, but her cult following is devoted. If we can get this place ready in six months, we'll need to book talent. You've gotten a lot of bad press this year but still came out on top. Mischa didn't press charges. No patrons were hurt at Debajo the night you two decided to bring your little fight club to town. Not that I'm complaining, but next time? Give me a heads-up so I can sell tickets."

My gaze snaps to Leni's.

I knew Rae was here when I decided to move this launch up the priority list for Echo, but she wasn't the reason. I was done hiding out in Ibiza, licking my wounds, and needed to get back to running a growing corporation—one ready and able to bury Mischa's once and for all.

"Not everything comes back to her," I say.

My friend crosses to me and brushes off my suit. "So, why did you have a check printed instead of having her final payment wired to her like the others?" She taps my breast pocket. "Don't worry, Harry. If I didn't know you so well, I'd have no idea you were still obsessed with her."

The check burns a hole in my breast pocket.

Through my suit, my shirt.

Possibly my skin.

When a member of Echo's team reached out to see where we could deliver the check this morning, Rae responded with the address of a studio lot. They purposely didn't say I would be the one coming.

The sun bakes my neck, my face damp under my sunglasses as I approach the trailer. The door opens, and two figures emerge—a young, athletic man with a woman slung over one shoulder and a stack of papers in his other hand.

The woman's curvy legs are encased in faded skinny jeans. One flip-flop falls off her foot, landing next to the steps of the trailer.

"You owe me a shoe," she huffs.

"Call my people," Beck replies cheerfully.

"Fuck your people. I'll stage an uprising in your closet while you're sleeping. Throw one of your five-hundred-dollar loafers out the bedroom window and see how much you like that."

The familiarity of Rae's low mutter is a kick in my gut. The feelings I've been shoving down rise up at once, colliding and combusting in a way that feels uncannily like heartburn.

"Excuse me, do you have ID?" A woman shifts out of a golf cart in front of me.

"I'm Harrison King."

Before she can stop me, I round the golf cart, leaving her behind.

"Well, this I didn't expect." Beck's amused, and his insolent drawl when he spots me has my nostrils flaring.

Rae shifts on his shoulder. "What's going on?"

"We've got company." He releases her, bending to set her on the ground with a thud.

It's an easy movement, as if they do this all the time.

I fucking hate it.

Rae straightens her top as she squares to face me.

She's the same as I remember... and different. Slow curves even understated clothes can't hide.

Dark hair tumbling over her shoulders, eyes framed with thick lashes narrowed in my direction so I can't read the emotion beneath even if I want to.

And I want to. I'd give every dollar in my damn wallet to know what's going through her head when we look at each other for the first time in a month.

It's been thirty-two days, actually, since I left her in my room in Ibiza.

That night, I wanted to stay with her but forced myself to carry out my duties as owner of Debajo and as a King. I went to see the police, then Christian.

Beck holds up the sheaf of papers. "I'm gonna go read. You need anything, I'm on lunch for another thirty."

She nods as he walks away.

Of the things I've pictured her doing since she left me, Beck wasn't one of them. Jealousy is a living thing in my chest as I consider what they were doing in that trailer together.

The possibility that he gets to touch her, gets to see her smile, gets to fucking *make* her smile...

It's agony.

Rae closes the distance, grabbing my jacket and tugging me to the side of the trailer as a golf cart flies by.

"What are you doing here?" she asks.

I drag my sunglasses off, tucking them into the pocket of my suit. What am I doing here? If I had a reason, it's lost in her eyes.

That's when I remember the envelope. "I was in LA for business and wanted to drop this off."

Rae's brows pull together as she accepts the envelope, opens it, and sucks in a breath. "This is more than my cut."

"We filled Debajo, which exceeded even my expectations. You deserve it."

Dark, troubled eyes search mine.

"Besides," I go on, impulsive, "I wasn't sure where to send the espresso machine, and you wouldn't use it anyway."

Rae shoves a hand through her hair, looking as if she can't decide whether to laugh or scream.

I want her to say she made a mistake by leaving. That she still thinks of me late at night after her shows.

Instead, Rae lifts the edge of my suit and tucks the envelope back in my pocket over my heart, her gaze lingering on my shirt as if she can see the scar beneath. "You don't owe me anything."

But it's the look she gives me before turning and starting back toward the trailer door—not angry but sad, overwhelmed—that steels me.

"You owe me something." She stops, and I

press on. "You left my bed without saying goodbye."

Rae turns slowly. "You didn't see the article?"

"I saw it. That's what happens when you're in the public eye. You grow a thick skin because the arrows only get sharper."

Her voice rises, her hands fisting at her sides. "I woke up to that news story, to the world calling me a hypocrite and someone I cared about shoving it in my face."

"Are you a hypocrite?"

"I don't know!" she retorts. "You didn't come back all night. I tried calling you. Waited for hours."

Each word is a knife in my gut.

I figured she'd decided I wasn't worth sticking around for, like everything else in her life. I wasn't going to reach out to her and beg her to reconsider.

The possibility she'd taken the article to heart never occurred to me.

She's so fucking young right now. It should be a warning, another brick in a fortress of reasons I can't have her, but all I want to do is drag her against me.

"You tried to reach me when I was at the police station," I say, clenching my hands into fists so I don't touch her. "I stopped to see Christian on the way home. When I got back, you'd left."

Raegan doesn't blink. "What about the issues with the clubs?"

"I swear I cleaned house. I told you I would make them better, and I did. There've been no issues since. Not a single claim."

She wants to believe me. I want her to, though I have no right to ask.

"The article made me question a lot of things," she says at last. "Things I'd stopped questioning while I was in Ibiza, playing for a man who was my enemy. One I swore I'd never support again."

"He's grateful."

Her eyes cloud, either at the expression on my face or the humility in my voice.

I won't beg. But seeing her like this, knowing where she's coming from, I need to make her understand.

I can live with being a villain, but I won't let her be one.

"I have somewhere to be," she says.

"I'll walk you out."

She reaches into the trailer, coming back with the same backpack she toted around Ibiza. The top is open, and I catch a glimpse of the contents before she flips the top closed.

"He can't do what I can do, " I say as we fall into

step next to each other and head down the road between studios, runners and golf carts passing every minute.

"I'll be the judge of that."

The clawing in my chest has my hands clenching into fists.

Hello, jealousy. It's been a while.

"Tell me you're not fucking him." I laugh, but underneath, I'm livid.

"That is every shade of not your business."

"It is because you still have feelings for me."

Rae pulls up, looking indignant.

"You kept the headphones I gave you."

She follows my gaze to the now-closed bag on her back, where I'd caught a glimpse of them in the sunlight. "They're diamond."

"And you live out of a single bag. You wouldn't want the reminder staring at you every day. So, if you were over what happened between us, you would've pawned them without blinking, love."

The endearment slips out, but I hide my surprise. She can't mask hers, though, and it's worth the mistake for the way she swallows hard.

When I talked with Leni, I was still telling myself I could move past Rae. Now, I realize...

I don't want to.

I resume my ambling toward the road until she catches up to me, her fingers digging into my skin through the jacket. This might be the first time I've wished I was wearing a polo shirt instead of a suit, if only to feel her touch without asking for it.

"What are you doing here, Harrison?" she demands. "You think you can keep an eye on me?"

"I purchased a lot in Burbank. It's an industrial warehouse I've been planning to convert to an entertainment venue."

"You're opening a new club."

"I need an act opening night. And whether you get off on my cock or just thinking about it"—her dark eyes flash—"you still owe me two favors."

"Not legally enforceable." Her voice is full of disbelief.

"But you're not a woman who goes back on your commitments. It's why you don't make them lightly. When you're done arguing with yourself, you know where to reach me."

I savor her stunned expression as I press the envelope into her palm.

It's hardly enough to tide me over until she comes back, but it'll have to do.

End of Sample

To continue reading, be sure to pick up *Beautiful Sins* at your favorite retailer.

THANK YOU

Thank you for reading *Beautiful Enemy*.

Harrison and Rae began as secondary characters in Tyler and Annie's story. Rae first appeared in *A Love Song for Rebels*, and Harrison (briefly!) in *A Love Song for Dreamers* (then did a little scene-stealing in *A Love Song for Always*...*cough*Jetski*cough*).

Their story has grown into so much more. In some ways, the relationship for these two happens on a bigger stage than Tyler and Annie's—not because they're more famous (infamous, in Harrison's case lol), but because they're dealing with not only personal problems but societal problems, too.

There are a lot of entrenched ideas about how to run a business, and where your responsibility stops and ends. I love that Rae challenges Harrison's beliefs about being a businessman, and a man. I also love how he pushes her out of her comfort zone, and sees who she could be.

So thank you for trusting me with your time and

your heart. And if you loved the sexy, emotional start of their story, you won't believe where it goes next in *Beautiful Sins*!

My readers are the most amazing readers anywhere. You guys are positive, bold, enthusiastic, supportive, and amazing humans. I wouldn't write without you.

If you enjoyed *Beautiful Enemy*, I'd be beyond grateful if you could take two minutes to leave a quick review wherever you picked it up. Reviews are like gold to us authors - especially indies.

If you do leave a review, I'd love to hear about it so I can thank you personally. Here're the best ways to reach out:
www.facebook.com/piperlawsonbooks
www.instagram.com/piperlawsonbooks
piper@piperlawsonbooks.com

Finally, make sure you're on my VIP list to get updates on news from this world! I always drop special giveaways and deals, too. You can signup at:
piperlawsonbooks.com/subscribe

Thanks for being awesome, for inspiring me, and for helping make it possible for me to do what I love every damned day.

xoxo
Piper

BOOKS BY PIPER LAWSON

FOR A FULL LIST PLEASE GO TO
PIPERLAWSONBOOKS.COM/BOOKS

OFF-LIMITS SERIES

Turns out the beautiful man from the club is my new professor... But he wasn't when he kissed me.

Off-Limits is a forbidden age gap college romance series. Find out what happens when the beautiful man from the club is Olivia's hot new professor.

WICKED SERIES

Rockstars don't chase college students. But Jax Jamieson never followed the rules.

Wicked is a new adult rock star series full of nerdy girls, hot rock stars, pet skunks, and ensemble casts you'll want to be friends with forever.

RIVALS SERIES

At seventeen, I offered Tyler Adams my home, my life, my heart. He stole them all.

Rivals is an angsty new adult series. Fans of forbidden romance, enemies to lovers, friends to lovers, and rock star romance will love these books.

ENEMIES SERIES

I sold my soul to a man I hate. Now, he owns me.

Enemies is an enthralling, explosive romance about an American DJ and a British billionaire. If you like wealthy, royal alpha males, enemies to lovers, travel or sexy romance, this series is for you!

TRAVESTY SERIES

My best friend's brother grew up. Hot.

Travesty is a steamy romance series following best friends who start a fashion label from NYC to LA. It contains best friends brother, second chances, enemies to lovers, opposites attract and friends to lovers stories. If you like sexy, sassy romances, you'll love this series.

PLAY SERIES

I know what I want. It's not Max Donovan. To hell with his money, his gaming empire, and his joystick.

Play is an addictive series of standalone romances with slow burn tension, delicious banter, office romance and unforgettable characters. If you like smart, quirky, steamy enemies-to-lovers, contemporary romance, you'll love Play.

ABOUT THE AUTHOR

Piper Lawson is a WSJ and USA Today bestselling author of smart and steamy romance.

She writes women who follow their dreams, best friends who know your dirty secrets and love you anyway, and complex heroes you'll fall hard for.

Piper lives in Canada with her tall and brilliant husband. She's a sucker for dark eyes, dark coffee, and dark chocolate.

For a complete reading list, visit
www.piperlawsonbooks.com/books

Subscribe to Piper's VIP email list
www.piperlawsonbooks.com/subscribe

amazon.com/author/piperlawson

bookbub.com/authors/piper-lawson

instagram.com/piperlawsonbooks

facebook.com/piperlawsonbooks

goodreads.com/piperlawson

ACKNOWLEDGMENTS

This story wouldn't have happened without the support of my awesome readers, including my ARC team. You ladies provide endless enthusiasm, cheerleading, and help spreading the word. I could NOT do it without you, and it would be a lot less fun to try. An extra shoutout to my Brit babes Suzanne and Anna for reading early! I needed you on this one.

Becca Mysoor, thank you for your story genius. Cassie Robertson and Devon Burke, thank you for questioning, polishing, and catching all the little things. Thank you Regina Wamba for the perfect image. This couple has been inspiring me for more than a year.

Thank you Dani Sanchez for your sage advice and for helping my stories find their way to the right readers. And Annette Brignac and Michelle Clay... I would not be able to get these books to the

people who matter most without you. Don't ever
leave me.

Last but certainly not least, thank YOU for picking
up this book. I love that you trust me to entertain
you.

Love always,
Piper